A
SLASH
In Time

A Novel by

Stephen A. White

1

PROLOGUE
London, England
November 9, 1888

Inspector Frederick George Abberline propped himself up against a dirty brick wall to steady himself as his stomach flipped and flopped like a fish out of water. It took every muscle in his body to keep from heaving up his early morning breakfast of porridge, fish, eggs and bacon. The rancid smells invading his nostrils were of no help in the dirty alley just off Brush Street, in the Whitechapel district of London's East End. It took all his will to breathe only through his mouth as the odor of garbage and raw sewerage assaulted his nostrils.

But it wasn't only the smell, as bad as it was, that made Inspector Fred Abberline physically sick; it was the scene he had just witnessed in a dingy flat at Miller's Court, which ran off Dorset Street. It was a flat rented by Mary Jane Kelly, a once attractive 25-year old woman. At least she would have been considered by many as attractive, until the killer known as Jack the Ripper had his way with her. What was left of Mary Kelly was lying on the bed. The scene in the room was appalling. Mary's throat had been slashed open, her nose and breasts cut off and placed on a table. Her entrails were draped over a picture frame. The body had been skinned and gutted and her heart was missing. Abberline was still shaken by the words of the rent collector who found her; "I shall be haunted by this for the rest of my life."

Abberline had seen some pretty horrible things since joining the Metropolitan Police in the winter of 1863, much of it while policing the streets of Whitechapel and Spitalfields. He wasn't a tall man—just a hair over five feet, nine inches—with dark brown hair, green eyes and a slight weight problem that would lead him to be described by those who met him as "portly." He had a thick mustache and bushy side whiskers. But no one doubted the 45-year-old detective's abilities as a criminal hunter. Which is why he was summoned to give an opinion of the murder of Mary Nichols, which took place on August 31, 1888, and who would become Jack the Ripper's first victim.

It was only the start. For three months in 1888, fear and panic would rule the streets of London's East End. During these months five women were murdered and horribly mutilated by a man who became known as Jack the Ripper. And the location of

4

these murders was of no surprise. Whitechapel was like a festering sore. The overcrowded population lived in hovels, the streets stank of filth and refuse, and the only way to earn a living was by criminal means, and for many women, prostitution. Abberline was familiar with the area, but even he couldn't predict the sordid and bloody path unwinding in front of him.

The body of Mary Ann Nichols, aged 42, was found in Buck's Row. Her face was bruised and her throat had been slashed twice and nearly severed. Her stomach had been hacked open and slashed several times. Abberline was barely into his investigation when on September 8th the second victim was found. She was Annie Chapman, a 47-year-old prostitute. Her body was found in a passageway behind 29 Hanbury Street. Her head was almost severed and her stomach torn open and pulled apart. Sections of skin from the stomach lay on her left shoulder and on the right shoulder, a mass of intestines. Part of the vagina and bladder had been carved out and taken away.

As a seasoned law enforcement officer, Abberline had to consider, in the wake of the similarities of the murders, that they came from the same hand. After consulting with his colleagues, it was determined that the crimes had been committed by one man, and not a gang. Whitechapel was now in uproar as riots broke out as hysterical crowds attacked anyone carrying a black bag as a rumor had started that the 'Ripper' carried his knives in such a bag. Things continued to spiral out of control.

The 30th of September was a grim day. The 'Ripper' carried out two murders within minutes of each other. Elizabeth Stride, also a prostitute, who was found first, at 1:00am, behind 40 Berner Street. Forty-five minutes later, the body of Catherine Eddowes, 43, was found several hundred yards away from where Elizabeth Stride was discovered, in an alley between Mitre Square and Duke Street. Eddowes' body had been ripped open and her throat slashed. Both eyelids had been cut and part of her nose and right ear were cut off. The uterus and left kidney were removed and entrails thrown over the right shoulder. Terror gripped London as rumors circulated, many of them unfounded; was the murderer a mad doctor, or even an insane midwife?

But what had been done to Mary Kelly was by far the most heinous of all the acts, and the one that threatened to push Inspector Abberline over the edge. The strain was starting to show; he hadn't slept in days, and when he closed his eyes all he could see were mutilated bodies. And sometimes they spoke to him, demanding to know why they had not been avenged. Abberline gripped the filthy wall tighter as his breakfast could no longer be contained.

As he wiped his mouth with his handkerchief, both ashamed and relieved that no one saw him get sick, a noise from up the dark alley caught his attention. At first he thought it might be a dog, or one of the many oversized rats indigenous to the Whitechapel district. On closer scrutiny he could make of the shadow of a man. But what caught Abberline's eye was the moonlight reflecting on something metallic in the dark figure's hand.

"You there, stop!" shouted Abberline. "I want to speak with you." But all Abberline's cry did was cause the man to turn and flee down the alley. Gathering up all the strength he could, Abberline started after him. Now breathing quite heavily, the

Inspector could see the figure, his cloak flapping behind him, hurry across Commercial Street and head down Church Street. The street was dark but Inspector Abberline saw the man enter a building at the end of the street. Advancing cautiously to the spot where the man went through the door, Abberline could see that it was the back entrance to a small store. A sign on the door read: **Madame Gau's Ancient Potions & Remedies: Deliveries Only**.

Abberline paused before entering, taking the time to pull out his pistol and ruminate on the wisdom of not calling for back-up. But time was of the essence; this he felt in his tired bones. Slowly he pushed open the door and entered the back of the shop. The room was dark, but the moonlight pouring in through the windows shone enough light that Abberline could see the room was filled with shelves housing various vials, bottles and jars. He walked as quietly as he could, although his beating heart sounded like a bass drum pounding in his ears. As he advanced to the end of a row of shelves, a black shape was suddenly in front of him. Abberline barely had a chance to discern what was happening when he saw a glint of metal flash in his peripheral vision. He cried out in pain as the knife slashed a three-inch gash above his right eyebrow, blood now seeping into his eye as he fell back against the shelf, the force of his weight causing numerous bottles to fall and shatter on the floor where he lay, as the dark figure started to move towards him. Suddenly, a strange green mist started to rise from the floor as the liquid contents of the broken bottles started to merge on the dirty floor. Through the mist Abberline could see his pistol, but now lacked the strength to reach for it as the strange mist engulfed him. Even as the world started to spin, Abberline could see that his assailant was being overtaken by the same mist, the knife now lying on the floor as he had likewise collapsed to the ground, choking and gasping for air. Then, Inspector Frederick Abberline's world went black.

While all this was unfolding, 80-year-old Madame Gau was working late in the front part of the shop, calculating the day's sales on her abacus. She jumped involuntarily when she heard the crash in the back of the store. Retrieving a sturdy piece of wood to use as a weapon if needed, as well as a kerosene lantern for lighting her way, and with her old bones creaking, she slowly pulled back the drapes that led to the dark backroom. She had anticipated that the disturbance was either caused by rats or someone trying to rob her. Madame Gau entered slowly, her trusty weapon at the ready. But all she saw was broken bottles, which was no surprise since she heard the crash. What did seem strange to her was that among the broken glass strewn about the floor there also lay a silver knife and a black pistol... nothing more.

There's a man in the shadows with a gun in his eye
And a blade shining oh so bright
There's evil in the air and there's thunder in the sky,
And a killer's on the bloodshot streets

-- BAT OUT OF HELL (Meat Loaf)

CHAPTER ONE
**Boston, Massachusetts
September 1, 2021**

Boston Detective Declan Maroney sat at his desk at Boston Police Headquarters on Mass. Ave, around the corner from the Boston Medical Center. He was slumped forward with his chin resting on his hands, which were placed flat on his desk. He sighed loudly as he surveyed the four pills lined up horizontally on his desk, like the front line of the New England Patriots. It was a good way to think about it; like he was Tom Brady (before the traitor defected to Tampa) and they were linemen protecting him from getting sick and maybe even dying.

He knew each one intimately; from left to right: Lisinopril (blood pressure), Simvastatin (cholesterol), potassium (what the hell was potassium anyway?), and Allopurinol (to fight gout). He stared intently at the Allopurinol, and then he scowled, thinking how that little white pill had betrayed him, which was the only way to account for his right big toe feeling like it was on fire. He winced at the ongoing pain and then opened his eyes and once again sighed, knowing—for full disclosure—that it was his own damn fault. He recalled how after taking in a Red Sox game last night with friends from another precinct, the decision was made to head over to Legal Sea Food near the New England Aquarium (*bad idea*). It was there—against all common sense for anyone that suffered the tortures of gout—that he decided to partake in a baked stuff lobster (*dumb*), shrimp cocktail (*dumber*) and clam chowder (*death wish*).

So now there they stood; The Four Horsemen of the HIPPA-calypse, taunting him because he had just turned 40, was about 20 pounds overweight, ate badly, maybe drank a little too much, and as a result he was now a slave to Big Pharma. And with that realization, he rounded up the pills, tossed them in his mouth and washed them down with a now-cold large Dunkin Donuts dark roast. And just to help ease the pain in his toe even a little more, he then popped three Tylenol, like some medicinal chaser. Sufficiently drugged and waiting for his toe to stop hurting, or at least lower its pain threshold, he put his head back down on his hands and thought about how he got to this spot in his life.

Declan Maroney had been a cop for the better part of 15 years. The first 10 were great; the last five—meh! The month he graduated from the Police Academy he married the then-Heather MacKenzie, whom he had been dating for two years prior. He felt they were a good fit, and they were, until they weren't, which is when the realization that they had very different backgrounds and very different goals in mind started to drive a wedge between them. Heather was from a well-to-do family that lived in a house the size of a small stadium in (*nose in the air*) Manchester-By-The-Sea, located on Boston's tony North Shore. Dec (as his friends called him) was from South Boston and decidedly lower on the social and economic scale. It became apparent as the marriage progressed (or maybe regressed was a better word) that they were drifting farther and farther apart, with no life-saver in sight. Declan wanted a family and Heather wanted a career, which she eventually got when she was hired by a local TV station to be one of its on-air anchors. Heather's drive to be the best at her craft, coupled with Declan's late hours as a Boston cop (adding to the fact that Heather's rich father hated him), led to a somewhat amicable divorce five years ago. Happily, though, they did remain friends. But, he had to admit to himself, he still missed her badly.

"Hey, Dec... you okay, man?"

Declan didn't have to raise his head to know the booming voice hovering over him belonged to his partner, Billy "Bear" Montour. "Bear" was six-feet, seven-inches and clocked in north of 260 pounds. He was Iroquois on his father's side and Irish on his mother's. His father, Matthew Montour, was down from Canada and working on a skyscraper in downtown Boston when he happened to meet and fall in love with the lovely Maggie Cullinane, who was working in a nearby industrial laundry on Harrison Avenue. They married and had a son, Billy, who would go on to become an all-state football hero at Catholic Memorial High School. Billy was offered a full scholarship to USC upon graduating from high school. But that summer, Billy's world changed. His dad was badly injured in a fall from a building he was working on in Worcester, and eventually succumbed to his injuries. Two weeks later Billy's Mom was badly hurt in an industrial accident while on the job, and lost the use of her right arm. The constant pain led to an addiction to painkillers and turned Billy into a full-time caregiver. Moving to California was now out of the question. Sadly, his Mom passed away a few years ago.

"I'm fine, Bear," Declan said, not bothering to look up as he spoke. "Except my big toe feels like somebody stuck it in a garbage disposal."

"Okay, Dec... a weird visual, but whatever you say."

"Why are you hovering over me like a super-sized drone?"

Declan could hear Bear rustling through the pages of his notebook. "A body, apparently very deceased, found at a swanky Beacon Hill townhouse... 442 Louisburg Square... by the homeowners who had just returned from two weeks in Paris."

"Texas?"

"No France. Apparently they hired some B.U. sophomore to babysit the house, feed the plants, to bring in the mail, and so on, while they were out of town." Declan finally looked up.

"Okay, anything else I should know? Any apparent cause of death?" Dec could hear Bear swallow hard.

"It's a bad one, Dec. Her face was badly bruised and her throat had been slashed twice, so badly it nearly cut her head off."

"*Jesus.*"

"Not only that, but her stomach... her stomach had been cut open."

Without saying a word, Declan Maroney rose slowly from his chair, put some weight gingerly on the swollen toe, and grabbed his sport coat off the back of the chair. Suddenly, a sore toe seemed like the least of his problems.

"C'mon Bear... time to earn our paycheck."

CHAPTER TWO
Boston, Massachusetts
August 31, 2021
Less Than 24 Hours Prior

The man sitting in the Aujourd' hui Lounge at the Four Seasons Hotel across from the Public Gardens was nursing a gin & tonic. Looking out the window he could see students, likely from nearby Emerson College and Suffolk University, dotting the grass, some tossing footballs and frisbees, others laying on blankets, engrossed in the upcoming semester's textbooks..

The man was of average height, trim and fit, perhaps in his late-30s. He wore beige khakis, slip-on loafers (no socks), a blue-striped button down shirt and a navy blue sport coat. His hair, and mustache and goatee were blonde; at least the ones he chose to glue on this afternoon (he had various shapes and colors available). He also wore a pair of tortoise-shell framed glasses, non-prescription, of course. His name was Allen Simpson, at least that was his name today, having chosen it after a popular cartoon series everyone seemed to be watching.

He took a sip of his drink and removed a picture he had folded in the inside pocket of his jacket. The photo revealed the face of a smiling, very attractive woman in her early-20s, with long brown hair and dark brown eyes. Her smile was radiant. The woman, named Bridget Dines, was a sophomore at Boston University. He had met her on a dating website called *LoveMeDo.com*, which Allen had discovered through something called Google (*what a ridiculous name*) was named after a song by some band from England. He still marveled at how some things in this world had perfect clarity, while others were like looking through frosted glass.

After a few online chats, they decided to meet at this bar. Allen took another sip of his drink and waited for Bridget's arrival. It would be a very special night.

A few moments later Allen saw a shapely young woman enter the bar and look around. She was wearing dark slacks, a white turtleneck sweater and a short black leather jacket. He knew it was her and stood and gestured. She saw him, smiled, and walked over. He held out his hand as she approached, "Allen

Simpson," he said smiling. "It's nice to finally meet you in person."

"Bridget Dines," she answered, her grip strong and assured. "Nice to finally be met." They both chuckled and took their seats. She ordered a Cape Codder and he another gin & tonic. And for the better part of an hour or more they talked about everything from her classes at school *(loved history, hated biology)*, his job as an investment banker on the South Shore *(thanks to info he found online since he didn't know a hedge fund from a hedge clipper)*, to how the Red Sox were doing this year.

"So, Bridget, other than going to baseball games, how are you keeping yourself busy this summer?" he asked nonchalantly. She took another sip of her drink (her third) and dabbed a napkin to her lips.

"It's been a great summer," she said with excitement in her voice. "I got a job babysitting."

"Children?"

"No, silly," she laughed, hitting his knee lightly. "House sitting."

"House sitting?"

"It's so-o-o-o cool! There's this rich couple who live in this *gorgeous* townhouse on Beacon Hill. And they went off to France, like rich people do, and they needed somebody to watch the place."

"Watch it do what?" he asked. This brought even more laughter.

"You know, watch it… bring in the mail, feed the cat, stuff like that."

Turning on his 100-watt smile, Allen feigned interest. "Wow," he exclaimed. "That's a great job. I don't think I've ever been in a real Beacon Hill townhouse before. What's it like?"

After having downed her third Cape Codder, Bridget was more than a little tipsy. She leaned in close, as if someone were listening in, and whispered, "They aren't coming home until tomorrow. Would you like to check it out?"

"I wouldn't want to get you in trouble," he said innocently. She just waved off the very idea. "They'll never know," she replied, fishing in her purse to make sure she had the key. "C'mon... you can also meet their cat, Kanye."

He helped her from the stool. "That's a strange name for a cat... never heard it before. Did they just make it up?," he asked sincerely. That made her laugh again , although he wasn't sure why.

"C'mon," she said heading for the door. "I'll show you how rich folks live."

CHAPTER THREE
Boston, Massachusetts
Beacon Hill
September 1, 2021

When Declan and Bear pulled into Louisburg Square they weren't the first ones on the scene by any stretch of the imagination. There were already several Boston Police squad cars in front of a three-story red-brick home, their blue flashing lights bouncing off the building's façade. There was also a coroner's van.

Parking their car along a courtyard that ran down the length of the street, they exited and navigated the cobblestones to the bottom of the steps leading up into the three-level townhouse. They flashed their badges at a uniformed cop who proceeded to copy down their badge numbers on a clipboard. Entering the house they found themselves standing in the middle of a massive dining area, with a long mahogany table being the centerpiece. Beneath it was a beautiful multi-colored Persian rug. There was a large fireplace with an impressive mantle; a painting hung on the wall above it. Declan didn't recognize it but had little doubt it was an original; a very expensive original.

Bear let out a low whistle. "Man, who lives in a place like this?"

"That would be Mr. & Mrs. Tobias Mendenhall."

Upon hearing the voice, both Bear and Declan turned to see their precinct commander, Lt. Molly Chin, standing in the doorway. She was dressed as always in black from head to toe, which went well with her jet-black hair, which was pulled back in a tight bun. She was one of the first Asian-American lieutenants in the Boston Police Department, and she quickly proved herself an intelligent and very tough boss. Declan liked her.

"Hey, Loo," he said. "Always nice to see you." And although she tried her best, Chin couldn't help but smile. "And you as well, Dec." Then her smile faded. "This is a bad one."

"So I heard."

She gestured for the two detectives to follow her into a separate living room, where the homeowners were sitting on the couch. They looked totally devastated; a glass of amber-colored liquid shaking in the woman's hand. Lt Chin made the introductions.

"This is Tobias and Rachel Mendenhall, the homeowners. Mr. and Mrs. Mendenhall; Detectives Declan Maroney and Billy Montour... why don't you tell them what happened."

Tobias Mendenhall nodded. He was a short man with a slight paunch. His hair was thinning and prone to a comb-over. He removed his wire-framed glasses, took out a handkerchief and wiped them slowly. His hand shook slightly as he put them back on and looked up at Declan and Billy. His wife poured another drink with an unsteady hand from a bottle on the table in front of them.

"Well, we had been traveling abroad for several weeks, mostly through France, and hired this young woman... Bridget.... to watch the house for us."

"When was the last time you spoke to her?" Declan asked.

Tobias had to think about that for a moment. "I think it was two days ago, when we were in Nice. We told her we'd be home today, about mid-afternoon."

"Okay."

Tobias continued. "When we got home the first thing we noticed was the door was unlocked. I didn't think a lot about it at the time; maybe she was in the house and expecting us." He paused and rubbed the top of his thigh, more a nervous gesture

25

than anything else. "We went into the kitchen, calling out her name a few times, but no answer. That's when Rachel noticed the wooden block holding the knives was tipped on its side. When she stood it back up she commented that one was missing."

"A knife?" Billy asked. Tobias nodded.

"That's when we knew something was terribly wrong," Tobias continued. "Then we... we... went into the bedroom..." And with that Rachel Mendenhall let out a cry, dropping her glass on the hardwood floor. "My god... my god...," she whimpered, burying her head in Tobias' chest.

Declan looked up at Lt. Chin, who gestured with her head for them to follow her towards the bedroom. They walked down a long hall and Declan could hear that the forensic people were already on the scene. There were numerous voices and the sound of a camera snapping pictures. Just outside the bedroom door, Lt. Chin stopped and turned towards Declan. She placed her hand lightly on his chest.

"Get ready, Dec... this is the place of nightmares," and with that she let the two detectives enter. Stepping into the scene, Declan Maroney could feel his jaw drop and his stomach flip.

Billy "Bear" Montour, all six-feet, seven-inches of him, let out a gasp and slumped against the wall.

Against a wall was a large four-posted bed, covered with a white sheet, or what was once a white sheet, the predominant color now being dark red. A woman, who Declan took to be Bridget Dines, lay on her back. She was wearing black pants and a white bra, also now red. Her hands were by her side and her legs were closed together. She could have been sleeping peacefully, had she not been horribly and obscenely mutilated. The pillow was resting beneath her shoulders which allowed her head to lean back, as if she were observing something on the ceiling with her open, lifeless eyes. This position allowed the gaping wound in her throat to give the impression it was smiling at Declan; it made him shiver. But as gruesome as that was, it was the ripped-open stomach, cut from left to right (or right to left depending on if the killer was right or left-handed) that was truly devastating. It was like looking through her, as you could see the coils of intestines and several other organs fully on display.

Staring silently at the victim for a full 10-seconds, Declan's eyes slowly drifted up to the wall above the bed. "What's that?"

he asked, looking at three letters, about a foot high each, scrawled in blood on the white wall.

MAN

Lt. Chin shook her head. "No idea…*MAN* .. maybe some kind of a message, or a clue… we don't know yet." Declan nodded slowly. "But it's something." He looked at Chin.

"Sexual assault?" he asked.

"No way to know as of yet," Chin said. "Probably unlikely, unless he replaced her clothes. Looks like this asshole got all his kicks *above* the waist."

"Okay, I want to be there when they do the autopsy. Who's the cutter?"

"Charlie Mitchell… just transferred in from Buffalo."

"Great," Declan replied, looking back at the body. "Tell him I'll be there." From behind he heard Lt. Chin softly chuckle. "What?" he asked, looking back over his shoulder. Chin just turned and walked out of the bedroom, answering without bothering to turn around, "Nothing, Dec... see you around."

Declan Maroney turned to look at Bridget Dines once more and shook his head. "Damn."

* * * * *

Early that evening, the crime scene at the Mendehall's townhouse now firmly wrapped up, Declan Maroney found himself traversing the gloomy corridors of Boston Medical Center's sub-basement, remembering it was one of his least-favorite places in the world. It gave him the heebie-jeebies with the dull overhead lighting, gun-metal grey walls, and what always seemed to be the sound of dripping water. The only thing missing was a loud alarm, swirling lights and some bad-ass ugly extraterrestrial and he could be an extra in *Alien 4*, or *5*, or whatever number they were up to these days. *UGH!*

Rounding a corner, he stood in front of a wooden door with a frosted-glass window, the lettering reading:

Dr. C. Mitchell

Inside he could hear the *whirr* of a saw as well as music which sounded like .... *ABBA*? Above the buzz of a saw he could make out someone singing... and it was actually not that bad.

> *Ooh, you can dance, you can jive*
> *Having the time of your life*
> *Ooh, see that girl, watch that scene*
> *Digging the dancing queen*

He opened the door and the music (and singing) got louder. Standing over a table (and what appeared to be the naked body of the late Bridget Dines), he saw what he took to be a female assistant to Dr. Mitchell, slumped over the body and diligently at work on the top of Ms. Dine's head while singing along to a CD, her very shapely backside moving to and fro.

"Excuse me," Declan said. But with the music and the singing he might as well be a mute. Sighing with frustration, he walked over and touched the woman on the shoulder... who promptly screamed and nearly dropped the saw she was holding. Declan jumped back about a foot.

"WHAT THE HELL...!" the young woman screamed, grabbing a remote and turning off the CD player. "You don't sneak up on people in a friggin' morgue!" she exclaimed, talking off her face shield and placing it on the table. "What's the matter with you!"

All Declan could do was stare at what he was sure was the most beautiful woman he had ever seen. She was perhaps in her late-30s, with short-cropped black hair, and big brown eyes that perfectly complimented her copper-colored skin. She stared back at him.

"Well, are you going to *say* something?" She gestured around the room where several tables held other bodies. "You know, I don't get a lot of conversation down here. So if you don't speak I will assume you are one of *them* and you *will* meet my saw." And to stress her point, she held it up.

"I'm sorry," Declan said holding up his hands, and finally coming to his senses. "I didn't mean to startle you. I said hello when I came in... but the music..." With that she turned away, seemingly embarrassed at being caught going full tilt karaoke in front of a less-than-enthusiastic audience.

"Well, it helps to kill the time," she replied. "What can I do for you?"

"I'm looking for Dr. Charlie Mitchell. Is he around?"

"SHE is around, and you are looking at her." Declan wasn't sure what to say, but he thought he detected a small smile on her face. "I'm sorry," he said sheepishly. "I assumed... but I guess I shouldn't have assumed. You know what they say about people who assume..."

"It's short for Charlene. And you are?"

Declan fished a business card out of his shirt pocket and handed it to her... keeping as far away from the saw as possible. "Detective Declan Maroney, Homicide, and that young lady" ... *he looked down sadly at Bridget's pale body...* "is my case."

The subject now brought back to the unpleasant task at hand, Charlie's anger slowly fizzled out. She also looked down at Bridget and sighed. "What a waste."

"What can you tell me, Dr. Mitchell..."

"Charlie... call me Charlie." She walked around to the other side of the body on the table, which now lay between them both. "And what I can tell you is she ran into one sick puppy." She took a pencil from her lab coat pocket and used it as a pointer, directing Declan's attention to the gaping wound in Bridget's throat.

"As you can see, the killer severed the omohyoid muscle, the thyroid cartilage, the trachea, both the internal and external carotid arteries, and the jugular vein," she said. "Damn nearly cut her head off. Is there any idea what the murder weapon was?"

"We think it was a kitchen knife," Declan replied, never taking his eyes off the wound. "There was one missing from the crime scene." Charlie nodded. "Could be; though it would take some strength to cut like that."

33

"Well, hopefully she was dead when he went to work on her stomach," Declan added, now glancing down at Bridget's midsection. "Christ."

"Interestingly, despite the savagery of the cut," Charlie said, "there is no damage to the internal organs. It's almost as if all he wanted was just a ... look inside." That made Declan shiver.

Declan jotted down a few notes on a small pad and put it back in his coat pocket. "Okay, thanks Dr. .... *Charlie*... if there's nothing else, I guess it's time to go to work," he said, holding out his hand. They shook over the body, Declan noticing how strong her grip was. "If there's anything else you uncover, please give me a call."

"I will... Declan," and as she said it, she frowned.

"What is it?"

"I just have a bad feeling."

"Want to share?"

Charlie looked down once again at Bridget Dines. "You know what all this feels like to me?"

"What?"

Charlie looked up at Declan, her lower lip trembling slightly.

"Practice."

.

CHAPTER FOUR
Boston, Massachusetts
September 3, 2021

For the next couple of days following the horrific discovery of Bridget Dines' mutilated body, Declan and Bear tracked down as many leads as they could find. They interviewed neighbors, talked to Bridget's roommates at B.U., and eventually were able to track her whereabouts to the bar at the Four Seasons the night she was murdered. They spoke briefly to the bartender on duty that night who conveyed the information that the man she was with appeared nice enough and they both seemed to be into each other. Declan took down the description of the man and continued the hunt for more clues. There weren't a lot; this guy was good.

Sitting at his desk staring at a computer that refused to yield any significant information no matter what he banged out on the keyboard with his two fingers, Declan sighed with obvious frustration. The database revealed no similar murders in the past 10 years… hell, in the past 25 as that goes. Maybe it was a one and done, he thought to himself. But Declan really didn't think so. If the game was finished why leave a clue on the wall? And what did it mean? He had Bear researching *M-A-N*, to see if it had been used at previous crime scenes, but nothing turned up. The other thing that stuck in his craw was Dr. Mitchell's—Charlie's—belief that this guy was just warming up. Actually, he found himself thinking of Charlie quite a bit; he was definitely smitten, he had to admit.

Looking up, Declan saw Lt. Chin approaching with two cups of coffee. She stopped and placed one on his desk. He nodded in appreciation.

"So, Dec," she asked, taking a small sip. "Where are we on the case?" Declan slumped lower in his chair, "Nada, Loo," he said. "Nothing similar in the database, and I have Bear working on what the message on the wall means. And I told you what Charlie said." Lt. Chin smiled.

"So, it's Charlie, is it?" she asked with a smile.

"Don't start."

Lt. Chin shrugged, "I'm just saying that it's been a long time since you dated. Maybe it's time to turn the page? She is quite attractive, don't you think?"

"I didn't notice," he replied unconvincingly. "And it's kind of hard to turn the page when your ex-wife is smiling at you on the news every night."

"Then just maybe," Lt. Chin replied, "It's time to turn off the TV and turn on your social life. I'm just saying."

"Maybe," Declan agreed. Lt. Chin finished off her coffee, crumpled the cup and tossed it into a waste basket next to Declan's desk.

"Keep me in the loop," she said walking away. "On everything. I'm heading home."

"Yeah, I'll do that," Declan responded, more to himself. "If and when I figure out what's going on."

* * * * *

Later that same evening, Dr. Charlene "Charlie" Mitchell, sat at the desk in her home-office of her 10th floor condominium in the Marina Bay complex in Quincy, Massachusetts, about eight miles south of Boston, going over notes from some of the cases she was working on, particularly the Bridget Dines murder. In fact, Charlie could see the Boston skyline rising across Boston

Harbor from her office window as dusk started to engulf the area.

Charlie loved looking out the window this time of day, remembering the words from "Dream On" by Aerosmith, because they explain, in some ways, why she is where she is today.

Every time that I look in the mirror
All these lines on my face getting clearer
The past is gone
It went by, like dusk to dawn
Isn't that the way
Everybody's got their dues in life to pay

Charlie moved to Quincy three months ago from Buffalo, right after her son, Ezra, graduated high school. He didn't seem to have any ambition about college, so the move was an easy one. And by now Ezra had seemed to get over the death of his father—Charlie's husband—who was brutally murdered on Christmas Eve 2020 while walking home from an office holiday party that Charlie was unable to attend because she was ill that day and chose to stay home.

The killer was never found, but the incident had a profound effect on Ezra, who suddenly delved into everything he could read about brutal crimes, particularly serial killers. He had become somewhat of an expert on the subject, and could recite verbatim anything you ever wanted to know about the Ted Bundy's and John Wayne Gacy's of the world. At first this infatuation concerned Charlie, until she came to the realization that he was using it as a coping mechanism for what happened to his father. Bottom line: he was a great kid. And as if on cue she heard the front door open. For the past few months Ezra had been working part-time at an independent bookstore in Quincy Center.

"Hey, Mom," she heard him call.

"In here, hon." She closed the murder book on her desk so Ezra wouldn't see such graphic photos.

The young man that entered the room and plopped himself heavily into a chair near Charlie's desk was short for his age and a bit on the pudgy side. His hair was kinky and shaping into a small afro. His skin color was decidedly lighter than his mother's, as his father was Caucasian. He wore jeans and a flannel shirt, unbuttoned, over a Captain America t-shirt. He held two books in his arms. Part of his job entitled him to a significant employee discount, which Ezra always took full advantage of. The bookcase in his bedroom was nearly filled to overflowing. Charlie sighed when she saw what he was holding.

40

"More books, Ezra? What is it this time; 'The Hannibal Lechter Cookbook'?"

"Ha-ha, you're hilarious."

Charlie smiled. "Okay, wise guy, show me what you have." And with that his face brightened, which only made Charlie smile even more.

"I've got this one," he said, handing the large paperback book to his mother, who read:

"*The Serial Killer: The Who, What, Where, How and Why of the World's Most Terrifying Murderers*," She rolled her eyes. "Charming."

"But this is the best one, brand new, just came out, hot off the press" he said excitedly. "Check it out!"

Charlie took the book; "*Dark Corridor: Inside the Mind of the World's Most Famous Serial Killers*, by Ian Kincaid." She handed it back to Ezra and asked, "What makes this one so special?"

"He's a local author, Mom, from Boston, and he's going to be doing a book signing at the store next Saturday. How cool is that!"

Charlie couldn't help but get caught up in her son's excitement. "Okay, bud, sounds like a keeper. Let me wrap up some things and I'll order us a large pizza." Ezra got up, and hugging his new prized possessions he walked over and kissed his mother on the head.

"Sound good... I'll be in my room. Don't forget the extra pepperoni."

Entering his bedroom, Ezra placed the books on his bookshelf, wherever he could find a spot, somewhere between *The Psychology of Notorious Serial Killers: The Intersection of Personality Theory and the Darkest Minds of Our Time* and *Unsolved Murders: A Stunning Look at Some of the World's Most Famous Unsolved Murders, Mysteries & Crimes: What Really Happened?*

The new books safely tucked away, Ezra sat on his bed and looked at the posters on his walls, all from movies featuring serial killers; *Silence of the Lambs, The Boston Strangler, Psycho* and *The Texas Chainsaw Massacre*, to name a few. He picked up his computer and put it on his lap, scrolling through his browser to his favorite website. It was a podcast called "Nightmare Ali" and the host—Ali Pendleton—frequently discussed stories about famous murders throughout history. But she also, somehow, had access to police reports whenever there was a murder in the city. He was hooked on it. As the webpage opened he saw the writer's face in the upper left corner. She was pretty in a Goth-y sort of way, Ezra thought. She looked to be about 25 years old, with short black hair embellished with thin blue streaks. Her face was pale and she had fingernails painted black. And to Ezra's delight, today she was posting a podcast about a recent murder on Beacon Hill. *Very cool!* He put in his ear buds and clicked on the icon on his computer screen, which happened to be shaped like a bloody dagger. Ezra leaned back on his pillow, closed his eyes, and listened.

NIGHTMARE ALI

Podcast #28

*Greetings all, this is your host, Ali Pendleton, and welcome to another chapter of **Nightmare Ali**.*

In today's podcast we'll delve into the darker inner regions of the mind of a serial killer. We'll touch upon the bizarre case of Mary Bell, who murdered two little boys in Newcastle, England in 1968. Was it because her mother tried to give her away and she felt unwanted? You be the judge.

And what hand does Ol' Satan play in the mind of a killer? Let's ask Elifasi Msomi. During a span of 21 months in the 1950s, this self-professed witch doctor butchered 15 people, most of them young children, in South Africa. When finally arrested in 1955, he claimed he was under the spell of an invisible demon that perched on his shoulder and told him to commit heinous crimes. Sounds to me like the devil made him do it. What do you think?

We'll discuss both these cases in tonight's podcast, but for something a little closer to home:

My sources tell me the Boston Police are currently working on a vicious murder that recently occurred on, of all places, super-rich Beacon Hill. Although the cops, led by Detective Declan Maroney, are keeping the details of the crime close to the vest, my sources tell me the victim was horribly mutilated. And the killer is still out there... who could it be? More details to come.

But now, back to our old friend, Mary Bell...

* * * * *

While Charlie was waiting for a Domino's Pizza delivery and Ezra was soaking up one gory story after another, the man responsible for ending Bridget Dines' life stood in his third-floor Kenmore Square apartment and stared out his window to the traffic going by on Commonwealth Avenue, likely heading for Fenway Park. Off in the distance he could make out several of the buildings on the Boston University campus as the giant CITGO sign flickered atop a building. The scene made him smile.

With his fake blonde mustache, goatee and hair safely tucked away in his bedroom drawer, he walked over to a mirror and gazed at the face looking back at him. He'd done this quite a few times over the past few months, with the full realization that he was a pretty handsome guy. He had brown hair, not too long, with thick eyebrows and dark expressive eyes. Someone once commented that he looked like an actor named Colin Farrell. The man searched on the computer (*a wondrous machine!*) found a photo of the actor and had to agree that there was some resemblance.

Love, love me do
You know, I love you....

The song kept playing in his head. When he first encountered the dating website with the weird name, it made no sense to him. But in the days that followed his satisfying time with Bridget, it started to become clearer and clearer, like a photograph that gradually comes into focus. The Beatles.... catchy tune.

This is the way the process had worked and he was gradually getting used to it. Some things automatically came into focus, like when he first sat down in front of a computer; his fingers seemed to instinctively know what letters to hit. Other's not as quick. He smiled as he remembered staring at a microwave oven dumbfounded for a week before he suddenly knew—PRESTO!—how to cook a frozen pizza in under a minute.

He was an uninvited guest, but he could have done a lot worse. He could have been a soot-covered chimney sweep, or a smelly fishmonger. Disgusting! He walked over to a small table near the front door and looked at the ever-growing pile of mail, all addressed to the same person. He picked up the one with the return address of *Bantam Books, 342 East 42nd Street, New York, NY.* He ripped open the envelope, took out its contents, unfolded the paper and read:

August 29, 2021

To: Ian Kincaid
Fr: Sal Dinsmore, Editor
Re: Book signing

Hi Ian,
Hope all is well.
This is to confirm your appearance at Hancock Street Books in Quincy, MA on Saturday, September 11, 2021, from Noon-2:00pm. We have shipped a carton of your books to the location, scheduled to arrive a few days prior to the event. Have fun!
Cordially,
Sal Dinsmore, Editor
Bantam Books

Ian folded the letter and put it back in the envelope. He looked at the bookshelf against the wall and walked over to survey the titles. He scanned the various authors, many of them unknown to him: Stephen King, John Grisham, James Patterson, C.J. Box (*Hmmm, that one sounds familiar.*)... until he found the book he was looking for. He took it from the shelf and looked at the cover:

Dark Corridor: Inside the Mind of the World's Most Famous Serial Killers, by Ian Kincaid

He turned the book over and glanced at the photo of the author on the back cover. It was like looking in a mirror.

Hmmm ... looks like a fun book, Ian thought to himself. And it probably wouldn't be a bad idea to actually *read* the book before the event, just in case there are questions. Ian made it a plan to read the book that night, but first he wanted to log on to his favorite podcast, "Nightmare Ali." He liked her voice and the subject she was delving into. "And," he thought to himself, "Maybe we'll even meet some day."

CHAPTER FIVE
Boston, Massachusetts
September 8, 2021

The man who was now Ian Kincaid was feeling comfortable in his new skin, no longer feeling the need to hide his identity with various disguises. After all, the plan had always been to have no witnesses. So why not take advantage of the good looks that have been bestowed on him.

He had quickly mastered the computer, and with a wondrous tool called Google at his disposal, he had discovered quite quickly why it was called a "search engine." He had found what he was looking for.

Google search: Best places to jog in Boston

In the short time he had spent in the Boston area, he found that for some strange reason young girls liked to run. Further research stated that the reason was to "get in shape," which baffled Ian because all the women he saw jogging, wearing as little as possible, looked to be in great shape. It fed his appetite.

According to his new friend Google, an area labeled 'the Jamaica Way" was a favored spot. And to minimize traffic, he quickly came to the conclusion that the early-morning hours would be the perfect setting. The previous day he had scoped out the area, making mental notes about how the jogging path was laid out, and noticed a short stretch that wound up a small hill and circled around what appeared to be an abandoned maintenance shack.

Now, as the sun started to rise, Ian Kincaid stood behind the shack in the shadows, his mind briefly drifting back to how comfortable he had always felt in the darkness, which somehow had always nurtured his hunger. It had also taught him patience; all good things come to those who wait. And patience would be the name of the game on this chilly September morning as he almost absent mindedly let his right hand caress the 10-inch blade in his overcoat pocket. He thought about the "Nightmare Ali" podcast and how the Boston coppers had begun investigating his last victim, focusing on one name in particular as heading up the investigation. The game is afoot, he thought, recalling it was something Sherlock Holmes once said in a book by his old friend Arthur Conan Doyle. He smiled slightly when he remembered their lunches together.

His mind now fully focused on the task at hand, he watched as several joggers passed by, including an overweight middle-aged man in sweatpants and a headband, already sweating profusely. Ian paid no attention to him, simply content in knowing he'll likely die soon on his own, probably by this afternoon. But his eye also caught something promising.

Coming up the path at a slow and steady pace, Ian could make out in the dawn's early light a young girl, likely in her 20s, wearing the briefest of shorts that revealed long tan legs and wearing what he had come to know as a jogging bra, shamelessly showing off large breasts. And for the briefest moment he felt a wave of disgust, as he once felt in the dirty alleyways. But it quickly passed. The young girl was now no more than 20 feet from where Ian lurked, all muscles in his body tensing like a tightly-coiled spring. As she came into the "kill zone" he leapt out. Perhaps she only barely caught the figure moving quickly towards her out of the corner of her eye, but either way she barely had time to react as Ian barreled full force into her, sending her sprawling heavily on to the grass at the side of the trail. By the time she recovered her senses, she felt herself being dragged to her feet, a beefy hand stifling her screams as she felt herself being dragged backwards. In her last moments on earth she would remember seeing one of her running shoes lying on its side on the path and wondering why it wasn't still on her foot.

Declan Maroney lived in a small white, two-bedroom house across from Wollaston Beach in Quincy, MA. He had found it after his divorce from Heather, who was now holding down a $4,000-a-month apartment in one of those ubiquitous high-rises that had popped up in Boston's Seaport area over the past five years or so. Declan enjoyed sitting in his living room, staring out at the ocean through a large bow window while sipping his first cup of coffee that morning. He had slept later than usual, having been out late handling a homicide in the Savin Hill section of Dorchester. It was now just a little after 9:30am and he was listening to sports talk radio streaming on his computer as the host, Greg Hill, broke down last night's Red Sox game.

Only half-listening to the game's recap while looking out at a few boats bobbing on the waves, his eye drifted towards his mailbox at the end of the driveway. And it struck him odd that the flag was up atop the box, something the mailman always did when there was mail in the box. And Declan knew without a doubt that when he pulled in the driveway around midnight last night, he took out the mail and lowered the flag.

"So if the mailman usually drops the mail at 5pm, why is the flag up at 9:30 in the morning?" he asked himself.

He surmised that, yes, it could have been done by kids walking by with nothing better to do. But that seemed unlikely.

Now, more intrigued than confused, he put down his coffee and ventured outside, taking a moment to breathe in the salty air before heading down his driveway. Once at the mailbox he opened it and saw a large, stained manila envelope had been shoved in. And without removing it he could plainly make out the letters inscribed in heavy black marker: **AC.** His stomach flipped as he walked back to the house to retrieve a pair of rubber gloves, knowing full well this was not a postal delivery. It was going to be a long day, he thought to himself.

* * * * *

Entering the morgue a few hours later, Declan saw that two homicide detectives from the 12th Precinct were already there; Detectives Mark Hannigan and Tito Gomez. They, along with

Charlie Mitchell, were looking down at the horribly mangled body of a young woman. They hadn't heard Declan enter.

"From what I can ascertain without going into a full autopsy," said Charlie, "is that the victim is in her early-20's, her head was close to being severed by the brutality of the cutting, her stomach slit and intestines pulled out, and some of the skin has been removed."

"Jesus, Mary and Joseph," Gomez said, letting out a soft whistle.

"Oh, it gets worse," Charlie added.

"How could it be worse than this?" Gomez asked, looking down at the body.

"There's also something missing," Charlie said.

"Missing?" Hannigan said.

"Not anymore," Declan replied, holding up the small plastic bag. Everyone turned to face him. "I found this in my mailbox this morning." He walked over and placed the bag on the table next to the body. Charlie carefully removed the contents and placed it on the scale. Hannigan and Gomez, both grizzled veterans of many horrible crimes, looked a little pale.

"What the hell is that?" Hannigan asked.

"The missing piece," Charlie answered, jotting down the weight on a pad of paper. "The victim's bladder."

Gomez took a step back, as if afraid the bladder was going to leap from the scale and attack him. "*Mae de Deus*," he murmured, blessing himself. Hannigan, on the other hand, elected to use comedy as his defense mechanism.

"I guess we found the killer," he said, attempting a smile. "Declan Maroney, you have the right…."

"Very funny," he replied. "What do we know?" Gomez composed himself and read from his notes.

"Victim is Carrie Goldstein, age 25, a resident of Allston, lives with her mother who is disabled; in a wheelchair. Body was found last night, around 11:00pm, behind an old maintenance shack along a jogging path on the Jamaica way. We think that's where the perp grabbed her."

Declan looked down at the body and shook his head. "Anything else?"

"Like what?" Hannigan inquired.

"Anything written on the shack near the body?"

Gomez and Hannigan looked at each other. "How the hell did you know about that?" asked Gomez.

"What was it?"

"Somebody spray-painted the letters **AC** on the wall of the shack, just above the body," Hannigan replied. "But that could have been done at anytime; maybe years ago." Declan shook his head.

"Don't think so." He paused and inhaled heavily, then looked up at the two detectives. "Listen guys, this smells like the same case Bear and I caught last week, and with that souvenir he left me, it's getting real personal."

"How did the perp know who you were, or your involvement with the case?" Gomez asked.

"I'm guessing my name came up on that killer podcast that everyone is talking about."

"My son listens to that show," Charlie said with a shudder. "It gives me the creeps." She waved her arms around the room. "And look what I do for a living."

"Anyway," Declan said. "I'd like to take this one on, if it's ok with both of you."

Hannigan shrugged, "Hey, it's all yours, boyo. I'll have my Lieutenant contact your Lieutenant."

Declan nodded and looked back at the remains of Carrie Goldstein. "Thanks… I think."

CHAPTER SIX
Arlington, Massachusetts
September 10, 2021

Ali Pendleton sat in a Starbucks on Medford Street in Arlington, MA, across from the Regent Theatre. Sipping her coffee and picking at a chocolate croissant she really didn't want, she glanced down at the laptop she'd been writing on for the past 30 minutes, showing notes for her next podcast. She wore her traditional short black leather jacket, black Metallica t-shirt and black jeans fashionably ripped at the knees. Her head bobbed slightly as her ear buds blasted out a Marilyn Manson song so loud it felt like her brain was vibrating.

She then switched her computer screen over to her last podcast and surveyed the comments below it.

Some were basic:

Donna231: Hey Ali… love the show. Keep up the good work.
Slasher123: Great stuff. Gruesome but great!
BettyBoop: You go, Ali girl!

Some were creepy:

MindBlower69: Love your podcast, especially while masturbating. Do you record it naked?

And some were just... strange:

RIPA88: Dear Ms. Pendleton, Just wanted to drop you a line to let you know how much I enjoy your podcasts and the obvious hard work that goes into it. I can tell by the research that you truly have an understanding of the mind of a serial killer. You never avert to sensationalism just to get clicks, as do most media outlets today. And I wanted you to know that we appreciate it.

("We?") Of all the comments, Ali had to admit that one creeped her out the most. She glanced at her watch and noticed her "date" was a few minutes late. She wasn't surprised; likely he took the long route around to avoid "being followed."

Ali's "date" was Danny Bolton. Just over a month ago, Danny had called her out of the blue and asked if she remembered him from high school, which she didn't, although the name was vaguely familiar. The picture became clearer when he described himself as thin, with freckles and a mop of red hair. He explained that he was now working in the records department at Boston Police Headquarters and had some secret information she might be able to use in her podcast. He also went on to explain that he was a huge fan of conspiracy and spy movies, about whistleblowers and the such, like in the movie *All The*

President's Men, and did she remember the scene with Robert Redford and Hal Holbrook meeting in the garage. Maybe it would be a good idea, he suggested, if they met on the top level of a deserted garage in Watertown at midnight. Since Ali never saw the movie, vaguely remembered who Robert Redford was, and drew a blank on Hal Holbrook, she came up with an alternative meeting site.

"How about Starbucks across from the Regent at noon?"

"Okay, that works, too. How will I know you?"

She sighed.

"I'll look like the picture on my website."

"Oh, right. But how will you know me?"

"You'll be the guy that sits down at my table." She was starting to get a little frustrated.

"Got it," he said. "See you then."

Now looking down at her computer, Ali had to smile thinking of the first meeting. Although completely paranoid, Ali had to admit Danny really was a sweet kid. And with that she looked up as Danny sat down across from her. His disguise today was a Red Sox cap pulled down on his forehead, dark sunglasses, and a wool scarf covering the lower part of his chin. His plan not to be noticed was kind of negated by the fact it was near 80-degrees outside.

"Hey, Ali."

"Hey, Danny." But before she could say more, a voice boomed out from the counter.

"I have a pumpkin spice latte with almond milk for... Sergei."

"I'll be right back," Danny said as he rose to retrieve his coffee. When he sat back down, Ali looked at him. "Sergei?"

"You didn't think I was actually going to use my real name did you?"

"Of course not. That could have been an FBI agent moonlighting as an $8.50-an-hour barista."

"Ha ha, funny."

Ali was starting to get impatient. "What do you have for me, Danny?"

Looking around; it seemed to Ali that Danny's head was always on a permanent swivel; he took a few sheets of paper from inside his coat and slid them slowly (and dramatically) across the table. Ali picked them up, glanced at them briefly, and her eyes grew wide. "Wow."

"Yeah," said Danny, "The Department is freakin' out about the killings, mostly just from the brute savagery of the acts."

"I'm not surprised. This is amazing stuff, Danny. Thanks."
She put the papers in her bag.

"What are you going to do with those sheets when you're finished with them?" he asked.

"I could eat them."

His face brightened.

"Would you?"

"No... but I will put them through a shredder."

"Great."

"Then I'll eat the shredding."

"Really?"

"No."

Danny shook his head slowly. "You know," he said. "I don't think you realize how dangerous this is for me." Was he pouting? She reached over and took his hand.

"I do... I *really* do." And with that he managed to produce a small smile.

"Thanks."

"Oh, and by the way," said Ali, dropping her voice and looking at a businessman working on a laptop in a corner. "I think that man in the gabardine suit is a spy." Danny looked over in horror. "And his bow tie is really a camera," she added.

Danny looked like he was about to jump out of his skin. But Ali just laughed. "Take it easy 007, it's just lyrics from a song my Mom used to listen to over and over." Danny visibly relaxed as Ali stood and collected her items. "I'm going to head out and work on the next podcast."

"Good idea," Danny pointed out. "Then I'll wait five minutes before I leave so people won't think we know each other."

"Except for the people who just saw us sitting here together and talking to each other for the last 10 minutes."

"Good point," he said with a frown. "Are you going to finish that croissant?"

"Have at it," she said as she walked to the door, pausing only to put a hand on his shoulder. "And thanks. This will be a killer show."

CHAPTER SEVEN

Boston, Massachusetts
September 10, 2021

While Danny Bolton was sipping his pumpkin spice latte and wondering if the pretty blonde behind the counter *could* actually be an FBI agent, Detective Declan Maroney was sitting at his desk at Boston Police Headquarters, depressed as ever.

The files for the last two murders lie open on his desk, the gruesomeness of the photos staring back at him, taunting him (*Catch me if you can*). He and Bear had zero luck trying to find witnesses or any useable evidence at the crime scenes. The killer was like a human vacuum cleaner; no traces of anything left behind. The only lead was on the first killing; an ID from a bartender. But Declan was willing to bet the house it was a disguise. And the newspapers weren't any help, with both *The Boston Globe* and *The Boston Herald* questioning why there had been no leads, as if this was an episode of *CSI* where the murder is wrapped up in one hour (less commercial time).

Looking up from his desk he hadn't noticed that Lieutenant Molly Chin was standing over his desk. "What do we have so far, Dec?" He rubbed his eyes.

"Same as before, Loo.... now only twice as much. Nada."

Lt. Chin tried to look sympathetic, but Declan could see by the frown lines on her face that she was getting squeezed by the top brass to come up with some answers. And she knew, and Declan knew, that it was only a matter of time before the FBI put their sticky little Fed fingers in the pie. For the FBI, serial killers were like catnip to a tabby.

Chin placed a book on Declan's desk. He looked down at it, asking, "What's this?"

"It's a book about getting inside the head of a serial killer. A local author. I want you to give it a read tonight."

"Aww, c'mon, Loo," Declan whined. "I have a date tonight with a big overstuffed chair, a Bud Light and Jerry Remy. Sox and Yanks." He picked up the book and attempted to hand it back. "Maybe I can just catch it when it comes out on Netflix."

Lt. Chin was already on her way back to her office, but not before yelling over her shoulder, "The writer is a local guy, and he'll be doing a book signing in Quincy on Saturday afternoon. Might be a good idea to drop by and set up a time to pick his brain. The more we know about our guy, the easier it makes our job."

Declan knew there was no winning this battle. He looked at the book in his hand. "*Dark Corridor: Inside the Mind of the World's Most Famous Serial Killers,* by Ian Kincaid," he read. "I guess everybody's an expert at something."

His thoughts were interrupted by the ringing of his cellphone, the caller ID identifying BEAR. He hit the receiver button.

"What's up Bear? Any good news?"

"Sorry, Dec," came the response. "I checked all over the Jamaica Way to see if there were any cameras, but nothing panned out."

Declan sighed. "That figures."

"Something else you should know," Bear said. "You know that podcast everyone listens to; the one about all the serial killers?" Declan vaguely did. "Something about an alley?"

"It's called Nightmare Ali... with an A-L-I."

"Whatever. What about it?"

"I just heard a promo that on tonight's episode they'll be revealing some juicy tidbits about the second murder that weren't on the news."

Declan fired a pencil across his desk. "Jesus Christ! Isn't our job tough enough? And where the hell is she getting all this info from?"

"I hear ya, boss… just thought you'd want to know."

Declan let out a long sigh. "Okay, Bear… thanks. Stay on it."

"Roger that." And Bear signed off.

All Declan could do was look down at his phone, now dead in his hand, and shake his head. "Damn," he said aloud. "Now I have to read books *and* listen to podcasts. When is any real police work supposed to get done?" And then he thought to himself, "And what type of timeframe is this guy working under?"

CHAPTER EIGHT

Quincy, Massachusetts
September 11, 2021

NIGHTMARE ALI

Podcast #29

*"Greetings all, this is your host, Ali Pendleton, and welcome to another chapter of **Nightmare Ali**.*

In tonight's episode we will discuss at length the strange case of John Eric Armstrong, also known as the "Psycho Sailor" because he served seven years aboard the aircraft carrier Nimitz. But once out of the Navy, he then turned to his newest hobby; butchering Detroit prostitutes in the mid-1990s.

And then we have our old friend Daniel Ray Troyer. This charming individual is said to have committed as many as 13 homicides in the late-1970s, in and around Salt Lake City,

Utah, starting with the killing of a 71-year old quadriplegic. Charming.

But first, we have some new local news that you might find interesting.

My secret sources tell me that the BPD has yet another brutal killing on their hands, as you may already know. It was a poor woman who made the wrong choice to jog by herself in the early morning hours out on the Jamaica Way. Apparently it was there that her killer pounced on her and brutally butchered her. However, what you didn't read in the papers, or in the police report, was that the victim was found, ah... missing something.

Tune in next week and we'll tell you exactly what the victim was missing. And even more astounding, where it was found!

But first, let's revisit the case of John Eric Armstrong..."

Declan's beefy index finger jabbed at the phone lying on the car seat beside him, disconnecting the recording of the podcast he taped last night. Listening to it twice was enough, because each time it just infuriated him more. When he finds out where the leak in the Department is coming from he'll ring the neck of whoever it is. He took some deep breaths and collected his senses, then took another sip of his large Dunkin Donut dark roast and glanced over at a half-eaten French Cruller sitting on the dashboard of his 2007 Honda Accord. He realized that he had lost his appetite.

It was a few minutes before noon and Declan was parked on Hancock Street in Quincy, not far from the Quincy Center stop on the Red Line and almost directly across the street from The Book Cellar. A light mist was falling and Declan's wipers set to intermittent cleaned off his windshield every five seconds. Still, he could clearly see that there was a buzz outside the store as a small crowd had gathered. The store's window displayed a huge poster, which was obviously the reason for all the activity.

BOOK SIGNING
Saturday, September 11 from Noon-2:00pm
Come and meet **IAN KINCAID**,
author of the acclaimed best-seller:
Dark Corridor: Inside the Mind of the World's Most Famous Serial Killers

The poster also featured a headshot of the author, and looking down at the back of the book Declan could see they used the same photo. Begrudgingly, last night Declan decided to read a few chapters (the Sox were getting their asses kicked by the Bronx Bombers), and he had to admit much of it was fascinating. He was never into the whole "profiling" thing, which had become a staple of the FBI over the past 30 years. But he reluctantly admitted; it was somewhat intriguing. Still, he wasn't sure how talking with a writer was going to help him capture a sadistic serial killer. But orders were orders. He looked at the photo on the back cover one more time and had to admit, he was a good-looking guy. He reminded Declan of that Irish actor with the thick eyebrows.... Farrell somebody.

After a few minutes, Declan drained his coffee and exited his car. Looking both ways to make sure he wasn't taken out by an Amazon Prime truck, he walked over to the book store and made his way through the crowd. Always using a cop's instincts, he decided to lay low at the back of the store where he could see what was unfolding in front of him.

Ian Kincaid sat at a table, stacks of his books on either side of him. The line to get a book signed was orderly and heavily skewed to the young female side. The author chatted amiably with his fans, signed books, and posed for a few selfies. A group of giggling girls passed Declan as they exited the store.

Declan noticed, standing slightly off to the side of the table, a young man with a slim build and a slight afro. He wore a name tag that Declan couldn't read from where he was standing, but he assumed the young man was an employee. Declan continued to survey the room and noticed a young woman standing off by herself in the corner, wearing all black. She looked vaguely familiar but Declan couldn't remember from where. The two hours actually went by fairly quickly, and as the last person in line thanked the author profusely, Declan decided now was a good time to approach. But just as he was ready to move, the young man with the name tag who was standing next to Kincaid sheepishly approached him, book in hand. Declan smiled at the scene as he could see the young man was truly nervous; obviously a fan. Declan decided to wait until Kincaid was done with the last signing.

* * * * *

Ezra Mitchell could feel his knees shaking as he stepped toward the table. His mouth felt dry. "Excuse me, Mr. Kincaid; I was wondering if you could sign my book?"

Kincaid looked up into his face and smiled. "Certainly... (*he looked at the name tag*)... Ezra. Is that who I should make it out to?"

"Yes, please."

Kincaid took the book, signed it to Ezra, and with a big swooping motion signed his name, dotting the "I" with a quick jab of his Sharpie. He closed the book and handed it back to Ezra. He held out his hand.

"It's been nice to meet you Ezra."

Ezra looked at the hand for a brief second then gripped it firmly. Suddenly a jolt of electricity exploded in Ezra's body and the room went dark for a split-second. But in that split-second a muddy image flashed in his head.

Then the lights inside Ezra's head came back on. The next thing Ezra saw was Ian Kincaid smiling and shaking his hand.

"Whoa there, hoss" said Kincaid, shaking his hand. "That is some serious static electricity. Maybe you better stay off the carpeting for awhile."

Ezra was still trying to clear his head. "What? Oh, I'm so sorry," he stuttered. "Ah, thanks for the autograph. But I better get going." Quickly Ezra headed for the door.

* * * * *

Standing at the back of the room, Declan saw the young man jump a mile when he shook Kincaid's hand. "What the hell...?"

He could tell even from this distance that the young man was very pale looking after whatever just happened and his hand was shaking, He said a few last words to Kincaid and fled the store like he was terrified. Declan thought little of the incident after that, guessing he was probably just excited about meeting one of his heroes. He figured now was as good a time as any to meet the man in person.

* * * * *

Ali Pendleton, dressed in her trademark black wardrobe, stood off in a corner of the store, thumbing through a Martha Stewart cookbook as if she were interested in purchasing it (*Yeah, right*). She glanced across and saw a middle-aged guy, with a trench coat standing in an adjacent corner, watching the book signing who seemed somewhat out of place. He was just standing there staring. Maybe he was some kind of a perv who knew there would be a lot of young girls looking for Kincaid's autograph or to take one of those annoying selfies. She then glanced at a young man standing at the side of the table; slim, short afro, kind of cute in a dorky way. He had a book with him and now that the crowd was gone he approached Kincaid for a book signing, which he graciously did with his killer smile. Then the weirdest thing happened. As the young man shook Kincaid's hand he seemed to leap out of his skin, like he just got hit with a taser. Kincaid laughed it off, but the young man looked both embarrassed and terrified. After saying a few last words to Kincaid he bolted for the door. As he left, Ali could see he was wearing a name tag. She thought it might be a good idea to ask the store owner who that employee was. It might make for an interesting chat.

* * * * *

Declan approached Kincaid who was now standing behind the table packing up some books. "Mr. Kincaid?"

Kincaid looked up at Declan. His eyes grew dark for a moment, as if registering something, but then suddenly brightened. "Yes," he said amiably. "One last autograph?"

Declan realized he was still holding the book. "No, not exactly." He flashed his police ID, which Kincaid leaned forward to read.

"Detective Declan Maroney." He looked up at Declan but the smile never left his face. "Am I under arrest?"

"Of course not," said Declan. "I just wanted to set up a time when we can talk about your book."

"My book?" Suddenly Kincaid was wary; did he screw up something? "What about my book?" His eyes quickly darted around looking for an exit. Declan didn't seem to notice.

"I am told you are somewhat of an expert at crawling around inside the mind of serial killers," he said. "And as you might have read, we have had a few killings recently."

Kincaid visibly relaxed but then it struck him like a thunderbolt. This was the cop that was mentioned on the killer podcast. The one leading the investigation. How grand!

"I have heard about those, Detective," Kincaid said, shaking his head slowly. "What kind of monster does something like that?"

"Well, that's what I'm trying to find out." He handed Kincaid one of his cards. "Maybe you can give me a call next week, and we can set up a time to discuss the situation with me and my partner." Kincaid took the card and held out his hand.

"It would be my pleasure to help the Boston Police in this grievous matter," he said, shaking Declan's hand firmly. "And it's nice not to get zapped by static electricity," he added laughing.

Declan smiled and thanked Kincaid for his time, turned and walked out the door. After he left, Ian Kincaid looked at the business card once again, put it up to his nose and sniffed it. He closed his eyes and smiled. Ali Pendelton, still lurking in the corner, witnessed the entire exchange and thought it was very strange. Along with electricity boy, she now needed to find out who that old guy was talking to Kincaid.

CHAPTER NINE

Quincy, Massachusetts
September 15, 2021

Charlie was worried about her son. Usually full of life and joking around, he was suddenly sullen and prone to remaining in his room as much as possible. She wondered if his obsession with serial killers and murders was affecting him. Maybe he should speak with somebody, she thought to herself. Ezra had also called in sick to work two days this week, though Charlie noted he didn't seem ill in anyway. As usual, he was in his room with the door closed. She had to find out what was wrong.

Charlie knocked on the door. "Ezra, can I come in?" No answer. "Ezra?" After a few moments there came an unenthusiastic reply. "Okay."

Charlie entered and found her son sitting up in his bed, a sketch pad balanced on his knees as he scribbled away with a charcoal pencil.

"Hey, bud," Charlie said. "What are you doing?" She went over and sat on the side of Ezra's bed. He just shrugged. "Nothing... doodling."

Charlie smiled, "Can I see?" When Ezra looked up at his mom she could see his eyes were red from crying. Maternal alarms went off."Honey, what's the matter?" She touched his arm.

"I don't know," Ezra said, his voice shaking. "A picture came into my head a few days ago and I can't shake it. Like it means something."

Charlie looked at the drawing pad. "Is that what you're drawing?" Ezra nodded.

"Can I see it?" Ezra hesitated, but slowly turned it towards his mother.

"Well, it is kind of creepy," she replied. "Could it have been something you saw in one of your books?"

"No, I saw it when I... touched someone."

"Touched someone," Charlie responded, trying to keep the concern out of her voice. "Who did you touch... or who touched you?"

"It's not like that!" Ezra said, his voice rising. "And I don't want to talk about it anymore. Can I please have some privacy!" And with that he closed the pad and placed it under his nightstand. He then turned over away from Charlie. "I'm really tired."

Unaware of what to say, Charlie responded softly. "Okay, hon, you rest." She patted his hip. "I'll check in with you later, okay." His answer was nothing more than a shrug of his shoulders. Charlie got up slowly, looked once more down at her son, and quietly left the room, closing the door behind her.

Ezra lay in his bed for another 30 minutes, thinking about what happened when he shook Ian Kincaid's hand. It had to mean something but it was something he wanted to find out on his own without dragging his mom into it. And, he had to admit, it was haunting him badly. Then, as if by fate, he got a notification on his phone of a text message. He opened the app.

AP: Hi, I got your number from your boss. Told him I was your cousin (lol). Saw U at the book signing, acting kind of freaked out when you shook Ian Kincaid's hand, like you saw a ghost. Would like to talk to you about it. Weird is kind of my thing. Can we meet?

Ezra just stared at the message. He didn't recognize the sender (AP?) But he had to admit he was intrigued.

EM: I guess so. Where and when?

AP: I am at the Panera across from the book store. How about 15 minutes?

EM: Are you a man or a woman?

AP: Does it matter?

EM: How will I know you?

AP: I'll know you.

Ezra thought about it some more. I don't know who this is. What if it's a killer luring me to my doom? After a few moments of serious rationalization, and then coming to the conclusion that it's unlikely there's a dude with a hockey mask and chainsaw eating a cup of broccoli cheddar soup at Panera, he threw caution to the wind.

EM: Okay, 15 minutes.

AP: Cool.

Ezra put his phone in his pocket, grabbed his jacket, and as he was about to leave the room, he stopped. Looking back at the pad under his nightstand, he went over and tore the page from the book and stuffed it in his back pocket.

"Mom, I'm going out to meet a friend for a little while," Ezra yelled heading for the door. His mother, who was sitting in a chair reading the latest James Patterson book, was startled by the quick change in demeanor. "What," she asked confused. "Where are you going?"

"Just down to the square," came the quickly reply as he opened the door. "Back soon ... love you." And with that he was gone.

All Charlie could do was stare at the door. Then, feeling a little guilty, she went to Ezra's room, where she saw his sketch book closed on the bed. She went over and opened to the page he was drawing in, only to discover picture's page had been torn out. Wherever Ezra was going, and whoever he was meeting with, the picture was a piece of the puzzle. Charlie sat down on the side of the bed and tried to put the pieces together in her mind.

* * * * *

Ezra opened the door and walked into the Panera across from the book store. Only half the tables were occupied, so it didn't take long for his to search for the person who texted him. His eyes stopped at a table in the far corner, where I young girl with black hair was holding up her hand and wiggling her fingers at him. She looked vaguely familiar. He walked over and as he got closer it dawned on him who she was and his eyes shot open wide. He stopped and leaned on the back of a chair.

"Oh my god!" he exclaimed. "You're Nightmare Ali!"

She smiled at him. "Well, yes and no," she said. "*Nightmare Ali* is the name of my podcast." She stuck out her hand and Ezra shook it. "But my name is Ali Pendleton. And I am pleased to see that I didn't get static shock like poor Ian Kincaid. Have a seat."

At the mention of the incident, and the reason he was here, Ezra's smile faded. Slowly he pulled out the seat and sat down across from her. "Yeah, well, that was kind of embarrassing," he said sheepishly. Ali waved it off like it was no big deal.

"But it was very interesting to watch," she said, picking at a corn muffin. "Tell me about it." Ezra looked down at the table, his hands clasped in front of him.

"I don't know, it was just weird."

"Like I said in my text... I am into weird. You've heard my podcasts, right?"

"Of course," he said, enthusiasm coming back in voice. "They are just the coolest thing ever. I love anything to do with serial killers. You should see my bedroom."

"Why Ezra," she said with a smile on her lips. "Is that an invite to your bedroom?"

"What? Oh, no!" he quickly responded, realizing what he said. He felt like his face had turned five shades of crimson. But Ali just laughed it off and patted his hand. "Only kidding." She could see Ezra sigh with relief. "So tell me what happened," she urged.

"Well, it was weird... and frightening," Ezra explained. "Like, nothing ever happened to me like that before." Ali said nothing, letting Ezra continue at his own pace. "When I shook hands with Mr. Kincaid, after he signed my book, it was like shaking hands with an electric eel. The sensation shot right up my arm, and suddenly there was a flash of light in my head followed by... by... like, an image."

"An image," Ali said. "Like, a premonition, or something?"

"It's hard to explain... but I still can see it in my head." He reached into his back pocket and pulled out the folded paper and put it on the table in front of Ali. She looked down at it. "This is a picture of what you saw?" Ezra nodded slowly. She picked up the paper and unfolded it, gazing at what Ezra had drawn.

"Whoa," she said softly. "Now that is creepy... even for me."

"What do you think it means?"

"I have no idea," came her answer. She looked up at him. "Has this ever happened before?" Ezra shook his head. Ali sat back in her chair. "Well, that wasn't the only strange thing that happened that day."

"What do you mean?"

"After you boogied out of the book store like you were being chased by Freddy Krueger, Kincaid was approached by some old guy in a trench coat. And they were talking for a while."

Ezra shrugged. "So, maybe he wanted his book signed."

"I don't think so," she said shaking her head. "First off, he didn't have a book with him. Then after a few minutes of chatting, the guy handed Kincaid his business card, like they were setting up a time to meet or to call each other." She smiled coyly. "And then I did a little snooping and guess who that old guy was?"

"I have no idea."

"Detective Declan Maroney."

Ezra wasn't sure what that meant. "Okay, so?"

"Are you saying you don't know who Declan Maroney is?" Ali asked, clearly perplexed. Ezra, now very embarrassed, just shook his head. But Ali's frustration gave way to realization and she slapped herself on the forehead.

"Of course you don't," she said. "Let me enlighten you. Did you hear my podcast on Friday night?"

"Of course… it was great."

"Thanks, I know," she said quickly. "Do you remember when I mentioned the last killing in Boston, and how I was going to reveal on my next podcast what the victim was missing and where it was found. You know, a teaser?"

"Yes, I can't wait until Friday to find out," Ezra said.

With that Ali smiled with great satisfaction. "Well, my good man, you are about to get a sneak preview… and (she lowered her voice for affect)… if you tell anyone what I am about to reveal I will kill you, chop up your body, and throw it in the Charles River." Ezra smiled; Ali didn't.

"Okay, I promise."

"Good," she replied. "Well, according to my secret sources, the item missing from the victim was… *her bladder*!"

Ezra could feel the blood draining from his face. "Her what!"

"Her bladder," Ali repeated. "And here's the best part; it was found in a mailbox outside a house across from Wollaston Beach."

Ezra gulped. "In a mailbox?"

Ali nodded enthusiastically, clearly enjoying the moment. "And guess whose mailbox it was?" All Ezra could do was shake his head.

"Wait for it... Detective Declan Maroney... the lead investigator on the murder case!"

"OMG," Ezra blurted out. "Do you think, do you think Ian Kincaid is... is a suspect?" Ali thought about it carefully for a moment before responding.

"No, I don't," she said thoughtfully. "Many people believe Kincaid, because of his book, to be an expert on serial killers. I suspect the BPD is just reaching out for any help they can get to solve the case. You know, profiling stuff."

"That makes sense," Ezra agreed. "Profiling is a hot button these days."

"Right," Ali said. "But I think I'll keep an eye on the situation." She looked at the clock on her phone. "Getting late gotta fly." She stood up. "Wai, how about a selfie of us, for my website?"

"Seriously?"

"Sure, come over to my side." Ezra walked over behind where Ali was sitting as she raised her cell phone. "Say Lechter," she said, taking the photo. She put her cell phone in her bag and grabbed her laptop.

"Nice meeting you Ezra… and remember what I said about not talking to anyone about this"?

"I won't," Ezra said.

"That's good," she answered while heading for the door, but not before placing a hand on his shoulder. "I wouldn't want you to be the subject of one of my podcasts."

Ezra wasn't sure if she was kidding or not. But what he *was* sure of was that Ali Pendleton was one very strange girl.

While Ali and Ezra were getting together in Quincy, the subject of their conversation—actually both subjects—were sitting in the office of Lt. Molly Chin at Boston Police Headquarters, along with Declan's partner, Bear Montour. Shortly after their meeting at the bookstore, Ian reached out to Declan and set up a time to chat, offering to help in whatever way he could. He had been invited in to talk and was now seated in front of Lt. Chin's desk, looking at notes and photos from the murders of Bridget Dines and Carrie Goldstein, as Declan and Bear looked on.

Ian shook his head slowly while viewing the information, conveying the message that he was saddened by the brutality. He looked up at Lt. Chin, "And you say he left some kind of… message at the scene of the crimes," Ian asked.

Lt. Chin looked at Declan, who was leaning against a wall. He said nothing, but his eyes conveyed what he was thinking. "Yes," she answered. "But at this point there are certain facts we have to keep private. I'm sure you understand."

"Of course," Ian said amiably. "I understand completely."

"So, Mr. Kincaid, any thoughts," Lt. Chin asked.

Ian sat back in his chair and folded one leg over the other, picking absently at a piece of lint on his trousers. He took his time before responding, giving the impression he was in great concentration, when in reality all he was thinking about was how great Lt. Molly Chin would look under his knife. Finally, he responded.

"Well, from what I see you are dealing with what I perceive to be a very intelligent, highly motivated individual. He is methodical and fully in control of time management, because what he is doing takes time. He is not a slash and run type of person. And he is planning out the perfect location, where he will be undisturbed in order to carry out his mission." Ian paused a moment, then continued. "I'd say he's probably in his 30s, maybe early-40s, physically fit, maybe even having undergone some medical training. Perhaps not a doctor, but certainly could be an EMT, or a nurse. Maybe even a veterinarian."

"And does this person seem like the kind of person who would keep killing," Bear asked, sitting on a sofa. "Can we expect more murders?"

Ian turned and looked at Bear. "Oh yes, Detective Montour. Most definitely."

"How can you be so sure?" Declan had to ask, though he thought he probably already knew the answer. This time Ian shifted around to look at Declan.

"Because a fish has to swim and a bird has to fly."

"What the hell does that mean?" Bear asked. But Declan knew the answer.

"Because it's what he was born to do."

Ian Kincaid nodded appreciatively. "Bingo," was all he simply added.

CHAPTER TEN

Quincy, Massachusetts
September 25, 2021

For the 10 days following the interview with Ian Kincaid. Declan and Bear tracked down every possible lead they could find, but it was becoming more and more obvious that whoever was behind these brutal murders was highly skilled at blending into the background. No one saw anything, no one heard anything, it's like he never existed, except there were two dead girls who would strongly disagree.

Understandably the entire city was on edge, a feeling of hysteria that the press says hasn't been felt in Boston since the days of the Boston Strangler. In his 15 years as a cop, Declan had never felt so impotent. And there was collateral damage. Lt. Molly Chin was transferred to another department, and the suits on the fifth floor were considering who should replace her. And of course, the Feds were always lurking on the perimeter, ready to pounce on the case at a moment's notice. They were like sharks smelling blood, and there was a lot of blood in the water.

Adding to the misery of the case were the podcasts that seemed to know as much about the murders as he did, which perturbed Declan to no end as he had yet to find out where the leak was coming from. Last week's was a doozy.

NIGHTMARE ALI

Podcast #31

"*Greetings all, this is your host, Ali Pendleton, and welcome to another chapter of* **Nightmare Ali**.

In tonight's episode we will discuss the strange case of Vincenz Verzeni. In 1871, "Vinnie" suddenly erupted in a bloody frenzy that resulted in two women having their bodies ripped open while he chewed on their flesh and drank their blood. Bon appétit!

And then we have San Francisco's favorite psycho son, The Zodiac Killer, who began his reign of terror by shooting a teenage couple to death in Lover's Lane on the night of

December 20, 1968. But we'll talk more about Zodiac, after this.

As promised, your host has come across some juicy information involving the recent murder of Carrie Goldstein and something that was missing when the body was discovered. Turns out, according to my secret sources, that poor Miss Goldstein had one of her organs taken, her bladder to be specific. Ew!! But don't fret listeners, the missing organ was found by one of BPD's finest, Detective Declan Maroney, who just happens to be heading up the investigation of the two murders. And where did the good detective come upon Miss Goldstein's missing bladder? Wait for it... in his mailbox! Now how cool is that!"

Every time he thinks about that broadcast he wants to punch a wall. Where the hell is that information coming from? It's not a departmental leak, it's a goddamn tsunami! He could see his knuckles turning white as he gripped his steering wheel with both hands. Fortunately he wasn't moving. He relaxed his hands and took a deep breath. From his car in one of the parking lots at Marina Bay he thought about the only good thing that had happened during the investigation.

During the time he had spent with Dr. Charlie Mitchell while working on the case, the more fond of her he was becoming. Finally, one afternoon he got up the courage to ask her out on a date. He had to admit he was crestfallen when she looked embarrassed and said she didn't think it was a good idea. But his spirits improved immeasurably when she suggested instead maybe he drop by for dinner and meet her son.

Taking a last look at himself in his rear view mirror, Declan grabbed the bottle of wine from the passenger seat and went to the front door. Quickly surveying the names on the mailbox he found MITCHELL. He rang the bell, identified himself, and gained entry into the building, taking the elevator to the 10th floor. Before he even had a chance to knock, Charlie opened the door. He thought she looked great, wearing jeans and a white turtle-neck sweater. She smiled at him and held the door open. He held out the wine. "I come bearing gifts," he said. "And hopefully you like it."

"Come in," she said pleasantly. "And I hope you like chicken parmigiana."

"Don't let the name Maroney fool you," he said. "I am a huge fan of Italian food."

It turned out to be an enjoyable evening full of good food and pleasant conversation (with no "shop talk"). Charlie's son, Ezra appeared extra quiet and distracted during dinner, as Declan tried unsuccessfully to recall why he looked so familiar. But once the topic of what Declan did for a living came up, Ezra's mood shifted considerably.

"Wow, you're a homicide detective!" Ezra exclaimed after they finished dinner and were sitting on the couch, drinks in hand. "That is so cool!"

Declan was flattered. "Well, I'm not sure cool is how I would describe it." But Ezra's enthusiasm would not be dampened. "Mom never lets me visit her at work," he said sullenly. "She thinks I would be traumatized."

"Your mom has a tough job," Declan offered. "It's not something I would want to do day I and day out." He looked over at Charlie who smiled back at him.

"I just love anything to do with crime and killers," Ezra said with excitement. "I like to try to crawl inside their heads and find out why the wiring suddenly went bad, you know?" But before Declan could answer, Ezra jumped to his feet.

"Mom, can I show Mr. Maroney my room?"

"Honey, I don't know…" But before she could finish, Ezra already had Declan by the arm and was pulling him towards his bedroom. "You're going to love it," he said happily. "You'll feel right at home. I like to think of it as kind of a serial killer museum!"

CHAPTER ELEVEN
Quincy, Massachusetts
September 30, 2021

Ian had the date circled on a wall calendar in his Boston apartment. He glanced at it briefly and then went back to his Facebook account. Well, technically it wasn't his account. It was for intent and purposes the account of Jimmy Doyle, a professional photographer who would be shooting the band on stage tonight for various publications, complete with a pretty cool photo he found on Google Images that he easily uploaded, complete with a bogus bio. But for the moment, Jimmy was talking online with a pretty coed named Catherine MacPherson about a Peter Wolf concert taking place tonight at the House of Blues on Lansdowne Street, across from Fenway's Green Monster, one that she and her BFF Sally Sanchez had tickets to attend.

The conversation really heated up when "Jimmy" mentioned he *might* be able to get the girls a visit to the green room after the show. This obviously created a deluge of happy and ecstatic emojis from Catherine, who Ian Kincaid imagined as a big fish wriggling on a hook.

Having already scoped out the venue, Ian was now quite aware that there was an alley behind the club that was rarely used except to house a dumpster and several rather fat rodents. He then explained to the very smitten Catherine MacPherson, that this was where the entrance was to the backstage area, and he'd meet her and her friend outside the back door when the show got over at around 11:00pm. Ian smiled as animated happy faces bounced all over his screen. He told her to enjoy the show and he'd see her afterward, making sure he got a photo of them with the boys in the band. Then he signed off and got ready for a big night.

* * * * *

Enjoying the real first deep sleep he had managed to get in weeks, Detective Declan Maroney lay in his bed dreaming that he was sitting on a faraway beach, sipping a pina colada, watching as Halle Berry and Nicole Kidman frolicked in the surf in the skimpiest of two-piece suits. In the distance he could make out the sound of Tchaikovsky's 1812 Overture, which he found strange because he expected to hear Jimmy Buffett. But Tchaikovsky just got louder... and louder...

When he opened his eyes he realized what he was hearing was the ring tone on his cell phone. Without lifting his head off the pillow he glanced at the clock on the nightstand. Nothing good ever happens at 2:00am someone once told him. They were right.

With no traffic to impede him, Declan made the trip from Quincy to Boston in a record 20 minutes. Exiting his car on Lansdowne Street, he glanced up nostalgically at the Green Monster, remembering back when he was a kid going to Fenway watching Ellis Burks and Mike Greenwell launch moon shots, back when there were no seats on the wall, just netting to catch home runs. But more seating meant more money for team owner John Henry, and so in 2003 the netting disappeared in favor of overpriced obstructed view seats where you couldn't see the left fielder if he was near the scoreboard.

Crossing the street he went around the back to the alley where there was already yellow police tape roping off the entrance. Declan pushed himself through a small crowd of drunken concert goers (many taking selfies), flashed his shield, nodded at the uniform on duty and ducked under the tape. Portable lights had been set up and the crime scene photographer was clicking away near a dumpster.

He walked over to where Bear and Lt. Molly Chin were standing, and when he did he saw a pretty girl lying on her back, open eyes staring up at the darkness. The front of her white blouse was drenched red where an ugly swatch provided an egress for what Declan figured was most of her blood. He just shook his head.

"Student ID identifies her as Sally Sanchez, a sophomore at BU," Bear said, reading from a small notebook. "Cause of death....well, you can see."

Declan shook his head and knelt down to take a closer look. "What a waste." He looked up at Bear and Molly. "You said there were two murders."

Bear swallowed hard. "Over here." Declan began to walk to the other side of the dumpster, but Molly stopped him with a hand to his arm. "This is a bad one, Dec." He looked at her and nodded, then went around to the other side of the dumpster. "Christ," was all he could think to say as his eyes took in what he saw.

Sitting up against a dirty brick wall was the naked body of Catherine MacPherson. Her eyes were open wide, staring, mostly because the killer had cut of her eye lids, as well as part of her nose and right ear. But that wasn't the worst of it. Along with having her throat slashed, she had been sliced from her chest to genitals. Her kidney lay on the ground beside her and her intestines had been pulled out and hung around her neck like some obscene scarf. Declan fought a gag reflex that threatened to empty his stomach. He held on to the edge of the dumpster to steady himself.

"From what we can ascertain," came the voice of Lt. Molly Chin. "The killer hid behind the dumpster as the two girls approached, he leapt out and quickly dispatched poor Miss Sanchez with one well-placed slash to the throat. With her out of commission, he now had ample time to work on Catherine MacPherson, who you see in front of you, also a BU co-ed." She then shone her flashlight a few feet above Catherine's dead staring eyes. "Plus, he had time to leave his calling card."

Declan looked up to where the flashlight was hitting the brick wall and saw two sets of crudely drawn letters:

ES

CE

All of a sudden that happy beach Declan Maroney just left seemed light years away.

CHAPTER TWELVE

Quincy, Massachusetts
Sunday, October 3, 2021

On a moon-filled Sunday night, as the last remnants of summer had given way to a chilling breeze that wafted over Marina Bay, Charlie sat in the living room of her Quincy condominium. On her coffee table a mug of hot chocolate spewed steam, and there was a half-eaten cranberry-orange muffin on a saucer beside it. The only other item on the table was Charlie's murder book. With every turn of the page, the photographs of the four young women brutally murdered by a sadistic killer seemed to haunt her. The photos and descriptions of the victims were vivid and graphic, spelling out in detail the severity of the wounds. The two murders several nights ago were still fresh in her mind.

Charlie wasn't sure why she kept a book like this, or why she chose to keep it in her home. Maybe deep down inside, although she obviously wasn't a detective, she felt she might discover some clue, a tiny piece of information, no matter how minute, that would help Declan track down this monster.

Declan. She couldn't help but smile when thinking of their "date." She enjoyed having dinner with him and the conversation never lagged. It was obvious he was attracted to her, although she wasn't sure just yet how she felt about things, and certainly she wasn't ready to jump back into a relationship. But he and Ezra got along quite well, and this was at least a box checked in his favor. Even if she just ended up with a new friend, she would consider it a win.

Stifling a yawn, Charlie felt her eyes starting to close and she realized it was just after 11:00pm. Ezra had gone to bed a little over an hour ago and she could detect the soft sound of his breathing in the next room. It made her smile. Downing the last of her hot chocolate, she fought sleep as an obstacle to finding the clues she needed. But she was losing the battle (remembering Edgar Allan Poe's description of sleep as "tiny slices of death"). Rather than give in to her drowsiness completely, she felt the best course of action would be to simply rest her eyes for 15 minutes or so, then continue her reading more refreshed. And with that she lay back on the sofa, determined to rest her eyes for only a few moments.

* * * * *

In her dream, Charlie Mitchell was trapped in a small cabin somewhere in the woods of New Hampshire. She was all alone with the windows boarded up and the door held shut by her living room sofa. She stood in the middle of the room, terrified, clutching her murder book as the sound of pounding came from outside the windows and on the door. She could see the sofa start to move back as the door was pushed open, heavily bruised arms protruded through the opening, the finger slowly moving like grass beneath the waves. Charlie opened her mouth to scream, but no sound emerged. Finally, with one large shove the door opened and what was once outside was now inside; the bodies of all the victims of the killings, slowly moving towards her. They were all naked, their bodies stitched in various positions, all sporting the "Y" stitching that ran from collarbone to pubic bone. They chanted her name slowly—"Charlie," "Charlie"—as they descended upon her, reaching for her as she slumped to the floor and used the book to cover her head. Finally, a cold hand touched her face…

Charlie sat up on the couch, her pajama top soaked with sweat, her breathing heavy. How long had she been sleeping? She rubbed her face slowly with both hands, trying to clear the cobwebs from her head, but stopped when she realized she was not alone.

Through the dim light of the room, she could see Ezra kneeling on the other side of the coffee table, looking intently through her murder book as casually as if he were thumbing through his latest comic book. If the sheer graphicness of the photos upset him, he didn't show it. He appeared to be studying each one carefully, occasionally flipping the pages back and forth, as if comparing one photo with the other.

"Ezra," she said softly. But he didn't answer, still seemingly fixated on what he was seeing in the pages. "Ezra," she said again, her voice a little louder. That seemed to catch his attention. He looked up at her quickly, and Charlie noticed his eyes seemed glazed cover, but they quickly cleared. Her son smiled.

"Oh, hi, Mom," he said. "Did I wake you?"

"Why are you looking through my book?" she asked, trying to keep the concern from her voice. "What time is it?" Charlie closed the book.

"A little after 2:00am," he replied. "I came out to get a drink and noticed you were asleep, so I put that blanket over you. You were shaking so I assumed you were cold."

"Thanks," was all Charlie could think to say, now remembering her nightmare. "But why look through the book?" And then to hopefully defuse a potential awkward situation she added, "You know this is what I do for work, right?"

"Of course I do," Ezra answered with some indignation. "I'm not a little kid." And then he seemed to think about it. "But I'm just curious why you have all these pictures?" Now it was Charlie's turn to look confused, but she tried to explain.

"Sometimes I try to help the Boston Police with their investigation," she answered, standing and reaching down for the book. "You remember Mr. Maroney."

"Okay, I get that" Ezra replied. "But what does Jack the Ripper have to do with the Boston Police?" Charlie stopped just as her hands touched the book. Bewildered, she looked up at Ezra, not quite sure what he had just said to her. "What?"

Ezra pointed to the book still sitting on the table. "This is a book about Jack the Ripper."

"Jack the Ripper?"

"Yeah, you know, the guy in London back in the old days, cut up hookers."

Charlie shook her head. "I *know* who Jack the Ripper is," she said, trying to keep the frustration out of her voice. "What does

107

my book have to do with that?" Now it was Ezra's turn to look confused.

"What I mean is, why do you have a book showing the Jack the Ripper murders?"

Charlie sat back down and looked at the book. She shook her head. "I don't understand."

With what Charlie took as a sigh, Ezra opened the first page of the book, the one showing the mutilated body of poor Bridget Dines. Slowly, Ezra read Charlie's notes on the case, which described in detail the severity of the wounds. He looked at his mother. "This is Mary Ann Nichols." He closed his eyes and thought hard. "Found murdered Friday, August 31, 1888 in Bucks Row, London, England." He turned to the next page, this one showing Carrie Goldstein, and Charlie could see his lips slightly move as he read her notes. When he was done he glanced once more at the gruesome photos. "This Annie Chapman," he said, pointing to one of the cadaver photos. "Killed September 8, 1888, her body found on Hanbury Street. Her bladder…."

"Okay, Ezra… *stop!*" She took a deep breath. Knowing her son's encyclopedic brain when it came to the subject of death, she had no doubt that he would identify the last two victims

108

along the same line. She forced a smile. "It's getting late... better head off to bed."

Getting to his feet, he went around and kissed his mother on the head. "Okay, goodnight Mom." And he headed back to his bedroom.

Unable to wrap her head around what she just heard, Charlie sat motionless for the next 10 minutes, her eyes closed and hands resting on the murder book, trying to determine her next step. But soon it was obvious. She grabbed her phone from the table beside the sofa and started to dial Declan's number, but quickly remembered in was 2:00am and he was surely asleep. She thought for a moment, and then quickly let her thumbs fly over the keys in her message app:

Dec, it's Charlie. I need you to meet me at my office at 9:00am on Monday morning. IMPORTANT!

She hit "send" and rested the back of her head on the sofa, staring up at the dark ceiling. "What the hell is going on?" she asked out loud to nobody in particular. She then walked over to her desk, sat down at her computer and opened Google in her browser, though she already knew the answer to the question she was asking herself.

CHAPTER THIRTEEN
Boston, Massachusetts
Monday, October 4, 2021

Declan was up early on Monday morning and read Charlie's message with some concern. He was tempted to call her back to see what was wrong but decided it would be best just to follow her instructions and meet at her office. He showered, shaved, got dressed and clipped the holster with his Glock to his belt, along with his detective's shield.

It had been less than a week since the last two murders (both on the same day), and just over a month since Bridget Dines met her demise, and still there were no real leads. The meeting with Ian Kincaid was informative, but shed no real light on the investigation. This guy was a ghost and trying to determine when he might kill again had become problematic since there was no real pattern to follow. The trail wasn't just cold; it was positively frost-bitten. Local politicians were outraged, the media called the Boston Police inept, and his Lieutenant was taking on more heat than a microwave pizza. The only constant was that all the victims were young girls. But that wasn't a big help.

After checking in with Bear at Police HQ, Declan headed over to Charlie's office at the City Morgue. When he entered he found her at her desk, staring intently at a book that he knew contained photos and details of the case. As he approached he could smell her perfume and his head swam for just a moment. He quickly collected his senses and sat down in a metal chair at the side of her desk. "So, what's up," he asked.

She looked up at Declan and he could see right away that she was troubled. "Early this morning I found Ezra looking through this book," she said.

Declan chuckled slightly. "Well, judging from what I saw in his room when I was over the other night, I doubt it spooked him much."

"It didn't," she answered. "As a matter of fact, he came up with a theory."

"A theory? About the murdered girls?"

Charlie nodded. "Yes," she replied. "As you know, I don't identify any of the victims in my book, but simply use initials."

Declan nodded.

"Well," said Charlie, pausing a moment to sip her Starbucks coffee. "He looked at all the photos, and the descriptions of the wounds, and he asked me a strange question."

Declan could tell after a few brief seconds that Charlie wasn't going to just go on without some prompting, so he asked, "What did he ask you?"

Charlie looked at Declan, her beautiful brown eyes staring intently. "He wanted to know why I was keeping a book about Jack the Ripper?"

Declan wasn't sure he heard right. "Jack the Ripper?" Charlie nodded, and then continued. "He said every victim was identical to the Jack the Ripper killings back in London in 1888." Declan wasn't sure what to say, so he said nothing. But Charlie wasn't through. "After I texted you last night I Googled Jack the Ripper on my computer and guess what?" This time Declan didn't hesitate.

"What?"

"The dates of our killings coincide exactly with the dates of the Ripper killings in 1888."

Declan thought for a moment before asking his next question. "Did Google mention if the killer left any lettering on the wall?" Charlie thought back. "No, I don't believe so."

Declan leaned forward with his elbows on his knees and rubbed his face. "So," he said slowly, "If Ezra is correct—and I don't doubt the kid—and Google is correct, then maybe what we are looking at here is a copy-cat killer. Does that make sense?"

But when Declan looked up waiting for Charlie's response, he noticed she was staring at the door of her office, which is where Declan heard a man's voice say, "Well, maybe yes, and maybe no."

The man standing in the doorway appeared to be in his early-to-mid 40s and was on the portly side. His face was clean shaven but sporting heavy side burns (what his dad used to call "mutton chops"). His dark hair was thinning and arranged in a comb-over that did little to hide the fact he was going bald. Declan also noticed a nasty-looking scar over his right eyebrow, which looked to be about three inches wide. The man wore blue slacks and a checkered grey sport coat over a black polo shirt. Declan surmised that fashion was probably not his strong point. Under his left arm, the man clutched a bruised and battered brown leather briefcase.

"Who are you and how the hell did you get down here?" Declan growled, rising to his feet. Charlie remained seated and said nothing.

The man didn't seem to be put off by Declan's gruff manner. He fished a business card out of his pocket and handed it to Declan, who reluctantly took it. He read the card.

"Joe Finn," Declan read. "And it says you're a Private Investigator from ... Gloucester."

"Originally from Portsmouth."

"New Hampshire?" Declan asked.

"England."

"Well, Joe Finn... you certainly have no trace of an English accent," Declan observed. "How long have you been in this country?"

Joe answered quickly, "A little over one month." Declan's eyes shot up. "Boy, you really lost it fast." But then Declan remembered his initial question and asked, "So, what are you doing here?"

"I went by your office this morning looking for you." He gestured to the other chair near the desk... "May I?" Declan waved his hand in the direction of the chair, acknowledging it would be alright. Joe walked over and sat down, placing the briefcase securely between his legs.

"They told me you were here and I came right over. I heard on that podcast (*Declan's face soured at the mention of "Nightmare Ali"*) that you were the lead investigator on the murders, and I thought I might be able to provide you with some valuable information."

"And what information might that be?" Charlie asked, speaking for the first time since Joe entered the room. "And what did you mean about maybe-yes, maybe-no when we mentioned it possibly being the work of a copy-cat killer?"

"Well," Joe said, pausing to carefully thinking about what he was going to say next. "A copy-cat killer mimics the actions of other people, in this case another killer."

"We know what a copy-cat killer is," said Declan, his frustration starting to show. "Tell us something we *don't* know or please leave. As you can see we're very busy."

Joe took a breath before continuing. "What I am saying is, can a copy-cat killer copy himself, and if he does, is he truly a copy-cat killer?" Declan started to stand. "Okay, that just gave me a popsicle headache. I think you better leave."

But interestingly, it was Charlie that spoke up.

116

"No Dec, let him explain." Declan looked at her curiously. Then he shrugged and sat back down. He waved at Joe to continue.

"Go ahead, you heard the lady. The floor is yours."

Joe collected his thoughts and knew he had to be careful about what he said, and how he said it, or else this was going to be a very short conversation. So he began.

"When I was in England I worked for Scotland Yard..." Declan interrupted; "You mean the NEW Scotland Yard," he said, referring to the name change in 2016. The question was met with a blank stare from Joe Finn. "There's a NEW Scotland Yard?" When Declan didn't respond Joe continued.

"Anyway, we hunted down a killer who was murdering prostitutes. We came close but never caught him. The press labeled him 'Jack the Ripper'."

"Because the killings resembled the MO of the original Jack the Ripper?" Charlie asked.

"There was no original Jack the Ripper," Joe replied. "It wasn't a copy-cat murder."

"Wait, I'm confused," Declan added. "Then how did your killer know how to commit the murders to resemble those of Jack the Ripper... when you say there was no Jack the Ripper at the time? Although we know from basic world history that there *was* a Jack the Ripper, running around the back alleys of London offing prostitutes back in 1888."

Joe closed his eyes and took a breath, knowing he had no choice but to state what he was about to state, and then wait for the blowback that was sure to follow. "What I am saying Detective Maroney, and Dr. Mitchell, is that the Jack the Ripper killings that I investigated in 1888, and your Jack the Ripper killings in 2021, are being committed by the same person."

The silence that followed was deafening. Joe waited patiently for a response.

"The same person..." Declan said.

"That you investigated..." Charlie said.

"In 1888..." they both said together. Joe nodded.

"Okay," said Declan, calmer than Joe expected. "Before I either throw you out the door or call the psychiatric ward, I have to ask a simple and pretty dumb question; why can't this just be some guy copying the Jack the Ripper killings? I mean, the description of the killings are all over the Internet; hell, Johnny Depp was even in a movie about it."

"Who's Johnny Depp?" Joe asked.

"Forget Johnny Depp; hasn't been in a decent movie since *Ed Wood*!" Declan yelled. "Don't you concur (*he looked again at the card*), Joe Finn, that *anybody* could figure out how to *be* Jack the Ripper, with all the information that's out there?"

"That's partially true, Detective," Joe conceded. "Back then the press, and, oh they were ravenous for information in London in those days, and very competitive with each other, pretty much had access to all the information about the killings. Sometimes they even got to the scene of the crime before we did. But we were very careful to conceal some small facts that were never shared to the newspapers, in the hopes that there would be a tip that would help us find the killer."

Declan dropped his head and just groaned. But Charlie was intrigued. "What kind of information, Mr. Finn?" Declan could see she was caught up in the story, probably still reeling from Ezra's revelations about the murder book.

Joe stared at her intently. "Let me ask you a question, Dr. Mitchell, when you were examining the bodies, did you check the bottoms of their feet, specifically the heels?" Charlie had to think about it for a minute.

"Well, no... there didn't seem to be a real need at the time. I mean, it was obvious from the severity of the wounds what the cause of death was." Charlie quickly realized she sounded like she was making excuses for herself. She looked over at Declan, who had nothing to add, but she could see by the expression on his face he was as intrigued by what Joe was asking as she was.

"Why do you ask?"

"Are the bodies still in your possession?"

"The first two have been released to their families, and I assume by now they have either been laid to rest or cremated."

"And the last two?"

"Yes, they are still with us."

Joe rose from his chair, still clutching his briefcase. "May I see them?" Charlie wasn't sure what to say. She looked at Declan for guidance but he just shrugged, his way of saying, "Let's get it over with so we can get rid of this nut-bag."

"Okay," Charlie said rising from her chair and grabbing a set of keys off a peg behind her desk. "This way."

Together they walked over to the morgue, which was only a few doors down from Charlie's office. Once inside she grabbed a clipboard that was hanging on the wall beside a row of steel drawers and used her index finger to find the location of the killer's two victims from last week. Satisfied, she walked over and drew out the drawer that revealed Sally Sanchez.

"Take a look at her heels, tell me if you see anything strange," Joe said.

Charlie did as instructed. She put her face close to the left heel and then the right, looking intently. Finally she said, "Sorry, I don't see anything."

"Okay, that's enough," Declan said, reaching for Joe's arm to escort him out.

"Wait," he said, moving away from Declan. After looking around briefly he saw what he wanted. He walked over to a table, grabbed a magnifying glass that was lying there and handed it to Charlie. "Here, look once more."

Charlie took the magnifying glass and looked at the girl's right heel. She glanced at Joe and shook her head.

"Check the other one." She did as instructed. Finally, after a good minute, she said, "I don't... wait. There does appear to be some kind of a mark...tiny needle punctures ... I think it's a ...."

"A star," Joe finished.

Charlie shot up. "How did you know that?"

"Please check the other victim." Charlie did and she discovered, incredibly, that Catherine MacPherson also had a similar mark—a star—on her left heel.

121

"Again, how did you know that?" Declan asked.

"Because," Joe replied. "Like most serial killers, our Jack the Ripper would make it a point to leave his calling card, his signature so to speak, kind of like a painter signing his name. He would use a pin and make the outline of a star on his victim's heel; marking them, so to speak. And I am pretty sure the first two unfortunates had the same markings... markings that only Jack the Ripper, and nobody else, would have been privy to; except, of course, the constables in London who first discovered his victims."

Declan leaned back against the wall. He was having a hard time digesting all this information. Charlie was speechless. Joe decided this was the time to try and spell out everything that was happening. In for a dime, in for a dollar.

"Who you see in front of you really is Joe Finn, a private investigator working out of a small office over a barber shop near the docks of Gloucester Harbor. I look in the mirror and that is what I see as well. Except for one small detail," he touched the large scar over his right eyebrow, "Joe Finn never had a scar." And to prove his point, he produced from his briefcase a passport which he handed to Charlie. She looked at it.

"This is your passport," she said. "I don't follow."

"Look closely at the photo, Dr. Mitchell, and the date it was taken." Charlie held it closer.

"It says the photo was taken when the passport was issued."

"Which was when?" She looked at the passport again.

"August 20, 2021."

"Right...and do you notice the area over the eyebrow... what's missing?" Charlie looked at the photo... at Joe... and then back to the photo. "There's no scar in the picture," she said.

"Exactly!"

"Big deal," pooh-poohed Declan, still not willing to concede anything. "You could have hit your head two weeks ago."

"Dr. Mitchell," said Joe, leaning towards Charlie. "Would you please examine the scar and tell me your prognosis of what you see." Charlie leaned forward to get a better look, letting her finger run over the surface.

"Judging by the healing, I'd have to say this scar is easily a couple of years old... maybe more."

"Thank you... now allow me to tell the rest of the story." Joe Finn looked at Declan for his approval... but was just met with a blank stare. He took that as an affirmation to continue. At least he wasn't sitting out on the sidewalk on his behind.

"On November 9, 1888, Inspector Frederick Abberline of Scotland Yard—a handsome fellow if I do say so myself—was called to a rooming house off Dorset Street on London's West Side. What he found there was unspeakable; horrors unimaginable. As Inspector Abberline was trying to come to grips outside the rooming house, he saw a dark shadow watching from the end of the alley; a man in a top hat and long cloak, or a cape, perhaps. It felt suspicious to him and as he approached the figure the man began to run, and Abberline could see the glint of a silver object in his hand, which he took to be a knife. After a brief chase he saw the man enter the back of a store, a store that sold ancient Chinese remedies. Cautiously, drawing his sidearm, he entered the store, where almost immediately the man attacked him. A struggle ensued, Abberline suffered a deep gash above his eyebrow (Joe touched the scar on his face) and both men crashed into a shelf holding dozens of potions in various sized bottles. The bottles crashed to the floor, the mixtures mingled, and suddenly a green haze filled the room. Coughing and attempting to catch his breath as the mist surrounded him, Abberline could see his assailant was undergoing the same discomfort. The Inspector was sure it was poisonous gas and that they both would shortly perish. Suddenly, darkness overwhelmed the Inspector."

Charlie found herself mesmerized by the tale. "Did he die?"

Joe just stared at her for a moment, and then replied, "Yes and no."

"What does that mean?" Declan asked.

"For all intents and purposes, Inspector Frederick Abberline of Scotland Yard—the *old* Scotland Yard—did indeed perish that night, or at the very least disappeared. But he is now known as Joe Finn; at least as of some six weeks ago. One minute I am running down an alley in London and the next I am looking in the mirror at someone I have never seen before, someone with no fashion sense and a bad hairdo, in a strange new world of computers, phones and reality TV shows. But strangely, as time went on these things became normal to me, like my knowledge of present day was lagging behind my actual inhabiting of Joe Finn's body. And it was easy once that happened to become aware of the murders that have taken place and then how to track you down, Detective."

"But what happened to the real Joe Finn?" Charlie had to ask, and Declan could see she was buying into this whole fantasy, although Declan had to admit it was kind of interesting. Joe just shrugged. "No idea. But I believe that whatever body I was to materialize in would have to at least have *some* connection to my prior life," he said. "I mean, I was a cop, and now I'm a PI. Not apples to apples, but pretty close. And I think the same principle applies to our killer."

"What do you mean?" Charlie asked.

Joe took his briefcase over to an empty table and started rummaging around inside. "Okay, this is where it gets really weird."

"Too late," said Declan. "That ship sailed hours ago."

Ignoring Declan's comment, Joe spread out copies of newspaper clippings. Unable to help themselves, Declan and Charlie ventured over to look. Joe was definitely caught up in the moment.

"I went to the Boston Public Library to research similar murders and what I found was fascinating," he said. "It seems that there were five identical 'Ripper' killings in 1921 in Spokane, Washington; 1954 in Chicago, Illinois; and in 1987 in Pittsburgh, Pennsylvania; pretty much 33 years apart from each other." Joe could see he had their full attention now so he pressed on. "And here's why I think whatever happens is similar to where I find myself today," he continued. "Although

126

no killer was ever identified in these cities, and the crimes never officially solved, every police report I read describes the prime suspect." He ruffled through the pages. "The key suspect in the murders in Spokane in 1921 was a prison guard on death row at Chandler State Prison whose job was to actually pull the lever that resulted in the hanging of hundreds of inmates. The suspect in Chicago in 1954 worked in the stockyards slaughtering cattle for beef. And, in 1987, in Pittsburgh, the prime suspect; a director of low-budget slasher movies." Joe tapped the papers on the table in front of him. "I believe that whatever that potion does, it finds hosts that at the very least, have a gene, or DNA or something that is inherent in that particular person. And it seems to happen every 33 years or so; like a giant time loop." He looked at both Charlie and Declan, who by now were completely dumbfounded, and then Joe Finn asked the question of the day.

"Does that sound like anybody you know? Because from what I can see, with all this technology available today, what with the Internet, dating apps on phones, Facebook groups, he has *never* had an easier time finding victims. He's like a kid in a homicidal candy store."

Without answering Charlie reached into her lab coat pocket and produced a folded piece of paper, which had the image Ezra had seen, which Charlie discreetly took a photo of with her cell phone while he was at work one day. She spread it out on the table and everyone looked down at it.

"What is this?" Declan asked, looking closely at the drawing." "It looks kind of familiar."

"My son, Ezra, drew it," Charlie answered. "Said he saw it in his head, kind of like a flashing neon sign, when he shook somebody's hand awhile back."

"You know what it looks like, don't you?" Joe asked, directing the question at Charlie. She nodded. "I do," was all she could think to say.

"So my question is this; whose hand did he shake when he had this... premonition?" Charlie shook her head, "I don't know... he wouldn't say."

"He doesn't have to," replied Declan, suddenly realizing why Ezra looked so familiar to him. Joe and Charlie turned to look at him. "I know exactly who it was. Wait... did you say *five* murders?"

Joe nodded. "Yes, there were five."

"When was the fifth one?"

Joe answered without hesitation; "November ninth."

"Shit! That only gives us five weeks."

"For what?" asked Charlie.

"To catch a killer."

* * * * *

That same morning, while Charlie, Declan and Joe were getting acquainted, Ezra sat on his bed and remembered the photos he had seen in his mother's book earlier that morning.

129

He recalled that each photo had been time-stamped with a date. It was one of the major reasons he thought of Jack the Ripper. Ezra's encyclopedic mind would rival Google when it came to any facts and figures having to do with serial killers. John Wayne Gacy; born March 17, 1942, kill count: 33. So remembering the Jack the Ripper murder dates was a no-brainer. But there was something about the dates that still bothered him.

This time he relied on the Internet to tell him what he needed to know and pulled up *The Boston Globe* website. After a little searching, he found what he was looking for; the dates of the last four unsolved murders in Boston. His mouth dropped open. They were the same dates that were in his mom's book. The photos weren't the Jack the Ripper murders. These were the current murders which, he surmised, must have been done by a copy-cat killer. But then a chill hit his spine as he recalled the image in his head, and what it looked like.

"Holy Christ," he thought to himself. He grabbed his phone and started texting, his fingers moving frantically over the keys.

EM: We need to talk ASAP!

After a few agonizing minutes, there came a reply.

AP: OK, when and where?

EM: The usual? 10 mins?

AP: OK, C U there.

By the time Ezra got to Panera, Ali was already in her customary seat in the back, pecking away at her laptop. She closed it when he sat down opposite her.

"Ok, what's so important?"

Ezra had to wait a moment to catch his breath. He held up his hand. "Did I ever tell you what my mom does for a job?" he asked.

"I don't think so... why?"

"She's a Medical Examiner for the Boston Police Department."

Ali's face lit up like a kid at Christmas. "No way! " she exclaimed. "She cuts up dead bodies!"

Ezra could see the conversation was threatening to go off the rails if he didn't keep it on track. He shook his head.

"No... I mean yes," he stammered. "But that's not the point."

"Then what is the point?"

"This morning I was up around two 2:00am, and my mom was asleep on the couch. On the table beside her was a book, so I looked through the pages." Ezra glanced around to see if anyone was listening. "And I saw all these photos of crime scenes, women horribly mutilated, with descriptions of what was done." He could see that Ali was caught up in the moment.

"Because I pretty much know more than anyone all there is to know about serial killers..."

"Hey!"

"No offense ... I could tell they were the Jack the Ripper killings; right down to the exact wounds."

Now Ali was confused. "Why would your mom have a book about Jack the Ripper?" Ezra shook his head.

"That's the thing," he explained. "Don't ask me why but for some reason the Ripper dates struck a chord with me, so I looked up the dates of the recent Boston murders online."

"And?"

"My mom's book wasn't full of photos of murders from 1888. They were murders from this year, 2021."

Ali sat back in her chair. "Suck a duck," she said. But then a thought occurred. "Hey, do you still carry that creepy picture around, the one you drew after Kincaid shook your hand?" Ezra fished it out of his pocket and handed it to Ali. She looked at it intently.

"You know what this looks like, right?" she asked. Ezra nodded as it was what he had been thinking about since first matching up the dates. He could see the wheels spinning in Ali's macabre mind. "So," she added. "We have a killer on the loose who thinks he's Jack the Ripper, and now we have a famous local writer who somehow did a Jedi mind trick on you and made you see...*she pointed at the photo*... Jack the Ripper when you shook his hand." She paused a moment for dramatic effect, then opened her laptop once more, letting her fingers fly across the keys. "Man, this is going to be one really great podcast!"

Ezra wasn't so sure. He was scared, and he thought she should be, too. "Ali, maybe you should be careful about what you write and say, ok?"

"Sure, sure," she responded, though never taking her eyes off the screen. Ezra just sighed heavily as rose and started for the door. But before he could take a step she called out to him.

"Hey Ezra, think you can get me copies of the photo's in your mom's book?"

Ezra never turned around or responded. He just dropped his head and slowly walked towards the door.

CHAPTER FOURTEEN

Boston, Massachusetts
Friday, October 8, 2021

NIGHTMARE ALI

Podcast #32

*"Greetings all, this is your host, Ali Pendleton, and welcome to another chapter of **Nightmare Ali**.*

In tonight's episode we'll get inside the head of Thierry Paulin, a man so depraved that in 1984 he killed an 80-year old woman by forcing her to drink bleach. Ugh!

And what about Danny Rolling a.k.a The Gainesville Ripper, who murdered five college students in 1990. Two of the victims were found with their mutilated bodies arranged in an obscene pose.

Speaking of 'Rippers,' it seems the recent crimes in our fair city have taken on positively Dickensian overtones, if you will.

My secret sources reveal that each murder was almost a perfect copy of those committed in 1888 by well-known London sicko, Jack the Ripper. And here's the best part. It's very possible that the police may already have an eye on a possible suspect, and it's someone with some local fame. Stay tuned for more details."

Driving in his car on the Southeast Expressway on his way home after another non-productive day, Declan Maroney almost drove off the road. He glanced at his phone on the passenger side seat and with a quick jab of his right hand disconnected from the podcast. He couldn't believe what he just heard. This chick knew about the Jack the Ripper connection, *and* who they were keeping an eye on. How was that possible?

No sooner had he disconnected from the podcast then a call came through his car's Bluetooth. He groaned inwardly when the caller was identified as Deputy Chief Frank Roberts. He pushed the button on his steering wheel. "Good evening, Chief."

"Don't good evening me, Maroney," came the growl over the speaker. "I have the Mayor on my ass wondering why he didn't know we had a suspect in mind!"

Declan decided he needed to try to keep what he knew as close to the vest as possible, especially with the Department leaking like a sieve. "Chief, I have no idea what that broad is talking about. I think she just makes things up to gather listeners." There was no response, which meant the Chief was considering the possibility.

"Okay, maybe… but what about this Zipper thing?"

Declan rolled his eyes and wanted to correct his boss, but that would just set him off. "There are some similarities that we are trying to connect the dots to, and once we come up with clear connections, we'll bring everyone up to speed." Again, Declan held his breath through the silence that followed.

"Well, as soon as you have something concrete, you let me know," Chief Roberts roared. "Understand?"

"Copy that Chief." And then he heard a click on the other end. Declan exhaled with relief, thinking that if he ever gets the chance he'd like to murder that podcast woman.

* * * * *

Declan wasn't the only person thinking about murdering Ali Pendleton. In his Kenmore Square apartment an enraged Ian

137

Kincaid slammed his fist down on a glass coffee table, spider-webbing the glass.

"I'll rip her fuckin' throat out!" he roared. "A sicko!" His chest heaved as deep breaths came and went. Finally, he started to get himself under control. He began to breathe more easily and closed his eyes for a few moments. When he eventually opened them he was more lucid, less emotional, and he realized the real problem with the podcast went beyond simple name calling. The problem was implying that the police had a suspect, and that the suspect was someone famous in the city. Perhaps he was overreacting; maybe Bill Belichick, or even Patrice Bergeron were under suspicion. But in his heart he could feel that she was on to something, possibly on to him, and he couldn't fathom how, or why. Still, it had to end. He could see the finish line in sight and he would not be distracted from his mission.

Killing the bitch would disrupt the order of things, so that was out of the question. Still, he thought to himself, she doesn't know that. So if he couldn't make Ali Pendleton go away, he could at least make her podcast disappear. Smiling, he walked over to his computer, still amazed at how easily you could pull up almost any piece of information, and researched just where to have a little meet-and-greet.

He quickly went to her website where he saw the usual photos of Ali with her adoring fans, selfies galore. But one photo captured Ian's attention. It was Ali with a young boy with a small afro. He quickly recognized him as the kid in the book store when he got zapped as they shook hands. What's their connection, he wondered? A little more navigating the sight, then a quick trip to her Facebook and LinkedIn pages, followed by her Instagram and Twitter accounts, and he had all the info he needed. As he shut down the computer, Ian continued to be amazed at how there are no secrets anymore.

Twenty-four hours later, Ali Pendleton took the few steps to the front door of her apartment on the first floor of a South Boston three-decker. Miraculously, in an area of Boston overrun by young people and what were once basic apartments were now being turned into million-dollar condominiums at monthly prices Ali could never afford, the old woman who owned this particular building refused to sell to the realtors who constantly circle her like hungry vultures. She lived on the top floor with her husband, the middle floor was occupied by an airline pilot that was never home, and the first floor was just Ali and her cat, Hannibal.

It was close to 9:00pm and she hadn't been home most of the day, so she felt guilty about not feeding her cat. As soon as she entered her apartment, even before turning on a light, she walked toward the bedroom calling for poor hungry Hannibal. But no sooner had she taken a few steps when a gloved hand clamped tight over her mouth, preventing her from screaming. Suddenly she felt like something pointed sticking into the bottom of her back.

"Hello, Ali," said a muffled voice. "You know who this is, don't you? Just nod if I am correct?" She did as she was told.

"Good... good," he said. "So, just to make a point, no pun intended, the pressure you feel on your lower back is a five-inch, very sharp ice-pick." With that her body stiffened and Ali let out a small whimper.

"Now," the voice continued. "All I have to do is exert a couple more pounds of pressure right in this spot, like so... *she gasped as he pushed the ice-pick in just a millimeter more....* And do you know what happens then?" She shook her head, tears now flowing freely.

140

"Well, Ali Pendleton, it's one of those good news, bad news scenarios you always read about. The good news is you likely won't die; there really aren't any vital organs in the general vicinity. The bad news is that this ice-pick will puncture your spinal cord in a very strategic spot, one that pretty much controls all your muscles and nerves from the waist down." She started to sob. "Which this time creates yet another bad news, good news situation." He was obviously enjoying himself. "The bad news is no more sex for Miss Ali Pendleton, which would be a great waste." He licked her ear and she shuddered. "But the good news is you might win a spot in the Special Olympics!" And with that he laughed.

"But, you know, we can avoid all these scenarios; and do you know how?" She shook her head. "It's very easy. You just stop doing your podcast. You go on next week, tell people… whatever. You're bored with killers, you found Jesus, you are looking to fulfill your dream to become a soccer mom… I DON'T CARE!" He pushed the ice-pick a little more. "But DO it! Those podcasts end today! Are we clear?"

Now utterly terrified, Ali nodded as much as she could. She felt the pressure of the ice-pick release.

"Good... very good. Now when I let go of you I want you to walk slowly into your bedroom, shut the door, and count to 60. If you scream or yell out, I may change my mind and decide it's just a lot easier to plunge this ice-pick into the back of your neck. Do you understand?"

She nodded. And Ian let her go. Slowly she shuffled to her room, her body shaking and tears now streaming down her face. As she touched the doorknob to her bedroom she heard him say, "And remember Ali... I can *always* find you." As Ian Kincaid slowly shut the door behind him, he began to think of the book store guy he saw in one of her photos. And wondered what the connection was?

CHAPTER FIFTEEN

Quincy, Massachusetts
Saturday, October 16, 2021

Ezra Mitchell's back ached as he lifted yet another carton of books and placed them on a shelf in the storeroom of his book store. The room was dark and musty, with floor to ceiling metal shelves, filled either with new product or old product being returned. Ezra thought to himself, you can read in the media all you want about how people are now choosing to download books on Kindle or Nook instead of actually reading books. But his aching lower back told him different.

Breathing hard, Ezra sat down on a box to rest, slapped the dust off his jeans, and kept wondering why Ali wasn't returning his texts. When he heard the door to the storeroom open he jumped up, thinking the last thing he needed was Mr. Sprenger, the owner, berating him. But Ezra quickly saw it wasn't Mr. Sprenger. He took a step backwards.

"Good morning," Ian Kincaid said pleasantly, a big smile on his face. "It's Ezra, right?" He took a few steps forward and extended his hand. Ezra panicked, and then held up his hands to show the dirt. "Sorry, pretty messy," he said with a grin. Ian's smile faded, but just for an instance. "Hey, no problem," he said affably. He looked up at the shelves. "Wow, they really have you working hard."

Ezra didn't respond. Finally, he said, "Is there something I can help you with Mr. Kincaid? Mr. Sprenger really doesn't like customers coming back here." Ian kept looking up and down the shelves, as if Ezra weren't even in the room. Finally he turned and looked at him.

"You're friends with that girl who does the podcasts, right?"

The question startled him. "You mean Ali Pendleton?" Ezra asked. Ian nodded as he again looked up and down the shelves.

"We're not really friends; I've only met her a few times."

"Hmmm," Ian said as he picked up a hardcover copy of Stephen King's mammoth *The Stand,* all 1200-plus pages. The book must weigh over five pounds but Ian handled it like a dime store paperback novel. He patted it against his leg and then turned back to Ezra.

"The few times you met her, as you say, what was the conversation about? You know, in general?"

"Conversation?" said Ezra. "I don't know, usual stuff, events in history, serial killers, like that?"

"Ah, serial killers."

"No, I mean yes, I mean that's what she does her podcasts about," he said quickly, trying not to stutter. His throat felt dry. "You know; her podcast."

"I see." Ian answered. "I've heard it a few times. It's beginning to interest me." He put the book back on the shelf and turned to look at Ezra. To Ezra, his eyes looked black. "You interest me."

Before another word was spoken the door opened. "Ezra, how is it going with that stock...?" When Mr. Sprenger saw Ian he stopped abruptly. "I'm sorry, I thought you were alone." Then he looked closer. "Ian Kincaid?"

"At your service."

"Can I help you with something? And by the way, thanks so much for doing our book signing." Ian clapped some dust off his hands.

"It was my great pleasure." Then he looked at Ezra. "And I hope to see you again, young sir." And with that Ian left. Mr. Sprenger watched him exit, smiled and shook his head. "What a great guy."

Ezra felt sick to his stomach.

When Ezra got home that afternoon, still spooked by the sudden appearance of Ian Kincaid, he frantically tried to reach Ali.

EM: WHERE ARE YOU? I have to tell you what happened today.

Not expecting an answer—and why should today be different than any other day—Ezra was surprised when his phone dinged.

AP: I need you to stop trying to reach me.
EM: Why, What's wrong?
AP: I'm going to be gone for awhile.
EM: I don't understand. Where are you going?

For at least a minute, Ezra stared at his phone.

AP: Goodbye Ezra. Be careful.

Ezra was stunned. He didn't know what to say. He started to text her back but thought better of it. Something inside him

made him turn on his laptop and pull up "NightmareAli.com".
In an instance a message flashed on his screen:

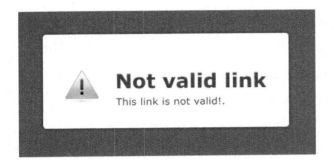

"What the hell?" was all Ezra could think to say. He typed
the URL again, thinking maybe he misspelled the name and hit
"Enter."

He sat back and looked at the screen, totally confused. His thoughts were disrupted by his mother coming in the front door.

"Ezra, give me a hand with these bags."

He went out and grabbed one of the bags his mother was carrying and placed it on the dining room table. "There's something strange going on, Mom," he said, handing her cans that she started to stack in the cupboard.

"Oh, like what?"

"Well, you know that girl who does that website I like?"

"I think so... Ali something?"

"Ali Pendleton." Suddenly Ezra wasn't sure how much he should say. "We kind of got to know each other; met a few times for coffee."

"That's nice," Charlie said. "Hand me the instant potatoes." Ezra did as he was asked.

"One time I showed her that picture I drew," he said. "You know when I got that image in my head when I shook hands with... someone."

"When you shook hands with Ian Kincaid at the bookstore." Ezra nearly dropped the can of cling peaches. "How... how did you know that?"

Charlie bit her tongue, not sure if she should have mentioned it. But it was too late to unring that bell. She turned and leaned on the counter. "Mr. Maroney was at the bookstore that day and saw what happened."

"He came by my store today," Ezra said, looking down.

Charlie was confused. "Mr. Maroney?"

"No, Ian Kincaid." Charlie stood up straight.

"What did he want?" There was no way to conceal the concern in her voice. "What did he say?"

"He asked if I was friends with Ali, and what we talked about together," Ezra said.

"Why did he want to know that?"

Ezra shrugged. "No idea. But she hasn't been answering my texts all week, and finally when she did she told me she was going away. I pulled up her website and the message says the website doesn't exist anymore." He paused to catch his breath. "Tell you the truth Mom, I'm a little freaked out and a little scared."

She went over and wrapped her arms around him. "It'll be fine, baby. Sit tight. I'm going to make a call."

CHAPTER SIXTEEN

Quincy, Massachusetts
Sunday, October 17, 2021

Less than 24 hours later Declan and Charlie were sitting on Charlie's couch, across from Ezra, who sat quietly with his hands folded between his knees. Occasionally, he glanced over at Joe Finn, who sat at the dining room table.

When Charlie went into the other room to call Declan yesterday, the conversation steered toward what they should and should not tell Ezra about what's going on, about what he could handle. But ultimately, because of his maturity and the fact that like it or not, he was already somehow involved, and apparently Ian Kincaid knew this, though it wasn't clear if he even knew Ezra was the Medical Examiner's son, it was agreed he would find out somehow, sooner than later. Thus, they would trust Ezra with the truth; which is why the decision was made to invite Joe Finn to be part of the discussion.

"So," Ezra said slowly. "You think what's going on with Ali has something to do with Ian Kincaid, and her podcast?"

"I think he scared her off," Declan replied.

"Why not just... you know?" Charlie said.

"Because we believe it would disrupt the natural order of things," Joe Finn added. Ezra glanced over at Joe, which he had done off and on since Declan and his mother explained what was happening. Now he couldn't keep it in any longer.

"Are you a time traveler, Mr. Finn?" he blurted out.

Joe looked at Declan and Charlie and tried his best to conceal a smile. Charlie just rolled her eyes. Declan thought to himself, "Kids, he wasn't even phased by the story."

"Well," Joe replied. "I guess so... in some ways."

Ezra could not be stopped at this point. "If Kincaid was all these different killers, then you must have been chasing him all those times. Do you remember it?"

That was actually a good question, one that Joe hadn't contemplated while all this was going on. "Hmmm, I don't know," he said. "Sometimes I see grey images, kind of in my peripheral vision, and then tiny slices of memory... I think I might have been a judge at one time. But I'm not sure."

Declan had a thought. "Ezra, when you shook hands with Kincaid you saw an image that we now think was Jack the Ripper. I wonder what you would see, if anything, if you shook Mr. Finn's hand.

"Dec!" Charlie said. "I don't think that's a good idea."

"It's okay, Mom," Ezra answered. "I was kind of thinking the same thing." He looked at Joe. "Should we try it, Mr. Finn?"

"Why not?" came the response as Joe extended his hand towards Ezra.

"Have you ever touched an electric eel, Mr. Finn?" Ezra asked smiling. Joe pulled his hand back slightly. "No, why?" He was suddenly less enthusiastic about the test.

"Just asking," Ezra said, as he reached out and clasped Joe's hand. Both of them shut their eyes... waiting... waiting... nothing. After a minute or so Ezra sat back shaking his head.

"Guess it doesn't always work." He actually sounded disappointed.

"Don't worry about it, Ezra," Joe said. "We are definitely sailing in uncharted waters here; there are no set rules to this game, no playbook to follow."

"Okay, enough with the magic tricks," said Declan seriously. "We need to figure out a game plan before November 9, which is only...."

"23 days from now," said Charlie.

"Right, and you can bet Kincaid isn't going to go on vacation for those 23 days," Declan said. "He needs a clean and clear path to his final kill, and whatever happens after that.

"That's the theory we're working on," Joe explained. "But it's all we have."

"Right," Declan agreed. "So what do we know and what does Kincaid know?" Everyone pondered the question for moment. Charlie was the first to respond. "He knows you're the lead investigator."

"Yes," Declan said. "He would have found that out even without Ali's podcasts. It's pretty much public record. But he doesn't know about the Bear."

"Who or what is the Bear?" Joe asked.

"My partner," Declan answered. "He's been working with me off and on since Day One, and we use him if we need an extra body."

"And Kincaid doesn't know that my Mom is my Mom," Ezra offered, suddenly realizing how dumb that sounded. "I mean, that she's the medical examiner on the case *and* my Mom."

"For now," Declan agreed. "But still, that's not an easy secret to keep."

"And we have Joe," Charlie said, "Which I don't believe he knows about either." Declan looked over and he could see Joe Finn in the midst of a deep frown.

"What's the problem?" Declan asked. Joe leaned forward on his chair, resting his arms on his knees.

"I'm just not sure how much help I can be," he said.

"Why do you say that?" asked Charlie. Joe sighed heavily.

"You have to remember; as young Ezra aptly pointed out, I've been down this road before, at least three other times."

"Yeah, so?" said Declan. Joe looked up at him.

"And the fact that I'm here today tells me I failed those other times." He lowered his head and no one spoke. But then Ezra stood and walked over to Joe and placed a hand on his shoulder.

"Don't think like that, Mr. Finn," Ezra said softly. "Like you said, there are no set rules, and what happens one time might not always happen other times." Joe looked up at Ezra and smiled. Ezra smiled back. "Maybe 2021 will be your lucky year." And with that Ezra squeezed Joe's shoulder a little tighter and suddenly both Ezra and Joe reeled back as a massive jolt of static electricity buckled Ezra's knees and Joe fell off his chair to the floor as an image flashed in Ezra's head:

"Ezra," Charlie screamed as she ran over and helped him to his feet. Declan did the same to Joe, who was shaking his head. "Wow!" was all he could say. "That was intense." Joe looked over at Ezra. "What did you see?" he asked.

Ezra closed his eyes and tried to collect his thoughts. When he opened them, he looked at Joe and asked, "Did you ever have long bushy sideburns?"

* * * * *

A few hours later, after really having no more success coming up with a plan, Declan and Joe left Charlie's condo in Marina Bay. Joe pulled his collar up to stifle a stiff autumn breeze while Declan gave Charlie, who had walked them down to the front

155

door, a hug goodbye. Declan and Joe shook hands and then departed for their respective automobiles. If they had taken a moment to look around, they would have noticed a four-door silver Audi parked in a nearby lot with its engine running, the driver peering at them through a small pair of binoculars.

Ian Kincaid watched the scene unfold from the front seat of his car. Knowing that Maroney was the lead investigator in the murders, Ian had taken it upon himself to trail the Detective whenever possible. Two hours ago he followed him to this residential building, though he wasn't sure why he was visiting. Now he was observing Maroney departing, but he wasn't alone. Ian looked closely at the portly individual standing with Maroney, whom he had not seen before. They obviously knew each other but what that connection could be was unknown to Ian. He would have to find out.

What he found even more intriguing, however, was Maroney's obvious connection to the attractive brown-skinned woman who resembled Halle Berry whom he just hugged, and who was now focusing on a young man who just appeared in the doorway and touched her shoulder... *whoa!* It was electricity boy! Most likely the gorgeous chick was his mom. Very interesting. Ian Kincaid would have loved to have been a fly on the wall for whatever was discussed upstairs. He would need to find out more about this woman.

But for now his interest was focused on the other guy. Who was he and what's his role in the game that's underway? Is he just an observer… or is he a player? And if he is a player; is it time to take him off the board? Ian Kincaid intended to find out.

He watched the man walk to a side parking lot and get into a black Honda Civic. As he pulled out, Ian followed, hoping the final destination was the man's home so he could keep close tabs on him, if need be. But the trip didn't end as Ian expected. After a short ride along Wollaston Boulevard, the man pulled into a Best Western hotel in the shadow of the Quincy side of the Neponset Bridge. An out-of-towner? Ian pondered the question as Joe exited his car, grabbed a small overnight bag and entered the hotel's lobby. Through the glass doors, Ian could see him checking in. Judging by the size of the bag, he guessed probably just for a night, which likely meant checking out in the morning. And with that, Ian made a quick call on his cell to the front desk, where he was informed that check-out was by 11:00am, and then departed for the short ride back to his apartment in Boston. But he looked forward to his return in the morning, and a conversation with Mystery Man.

* * * * *

Joe Finn, having chosen not to drive back to Gloucester yesterday, was up by 9:00am and having finished breakfast in the hotel lobby, now grabbed his overnight bag and headed out to his car which was parked facing the chilly Neponset River. The sky was dark and overcast and somehow Indian Summer never showed up this year.

The only other car in the area was a very cool-looking silver Audi parked two spaces over from him, its trunk open and the driver apparently rummaging around inside looking for something. His back was to Joe. Not thinking further about it, Joe unlocked his car and opened the door. But before he could get in, a strong hand clamped over his mouth and what felt like a sharp blade was placed on his throat.

"You don't want to move too much," said the calm voice behind him. "This is a very sharp blade and it would not take much to slice through your jugular. Do you understand? Nod if yes." Joe nodded once, slowly, not willing to have his movements interact with the blade.

"Very good. Now hand me the keys over your shoulder... slowly." Joe did as instructed. The blade moved temporarily from his throat as he heard the back door being opened on the driver's side. Then the blade returned. "Now get in and place both hands on the steering wheel. I am going to get in behind you. Any sudden movement... yelling out or leaning on the horn... I guarantee no one will come to your rescue in the time it takes me to cut all the way through to your spine. Understood?" Joe nodded again.

"Good... get in. And shut the door with your left hand, then put it back on the wheel." As Joe was doing as instructed, he heard the man get in behind him and quickly shut his door and in mere seconds Joe felt the blade on his throat once again. He swallowed hard. He glanced quickly at his rearview mirror but the figure in the back seat was too far over behind him to get a

159

good look. But he had a pretty good idea who was in the back seat, Joe decided he needed to take the offensive.

"Look," Joe said. "I don't have a lot of money on me; maybe fifty bucks. Just take it."

The man behind him snickered. "Is that what you think this is… a robbery? Like some petty common thief? I'm not here for money."

"Then what is it you want?"

"Information. Who are you?"

"What do you mean?" Joe tensed as the knife pushed slightly into his throat.

"Don't screw with me!" the man snarled.

"My name is Joe Finn." He felt the knife relax against his throat.

"And what do you do for work, Joe Finn?"

"I'm a salesman… electrical parts. Work for a company up on the North Shore."

"Hmmm… and how do you know Detective Declan Maroney?"

So that's it, Joe thought to himself, he saw us leave the condo together. He had to think fast. "We went to college together, Suffolk University, class of 2003. Go Rams! We hadn't seen each other for quite awhile so I gave him a call, asked if he wanted to get together." Joe waited for a response. The knife didn't move.

"Hmmm … so why meet in that building?" asked the voice in the backseat. "I know he doesn't live there."

Joe's mind was racing as he was making this up on the fly. "It's his girlfriend's apartment. He mentioned meeting there so he could introduce her to me. She seemed nice. Pretty lady. Looks a lot like Halle Berry, don't you think?"

A few tense minutes passed. The knife never wavered. Joe continued to stare straight ahead.

161

"And the young man I saw; was that her son?"

Damn! He saw Ezra. Joe saw no sense in a denial. "Yes. That was her son." He could hear the sounds of people walking by, talking amongst themselves.

"Hmmm... okay Joe Finn. We'll table this discussion for later when we have a little more privacy. Have a good sleep."

"What do you mean have ..." But before he could finish his sentence, he felt a damp cloth clamp over his nose and mouth, a sticky-sweet smell going up his nostrils. His head began to swim as darkness engulfed him and he slumped over on to the passenger seat.

Two hours later Joe struggled to sit up. His mouth was dry and his head ached. When he finally opened his eyes he saw his car keys on the dashboard. He put his window down and let the cool October air wash over him. He breathed in deeply and immediately started to feel better. He took out his phone and dialed Declan Maroney. It only rang twice.

"Maroney," he said curtly, like he was concentrating on other matters.

"Finn. Guess who I just had a chat with?"

"Nicole Kidman."

"I think I know who that is," he replied. "But I'm not sure."

"I'm getting bored."

"Our friend. The blast from the past." Now Joe knew he had Declan's full attention.

"What? Where? Are you ok?"

"I'm not sure there's an answer to 'what,' but the 'where' is the parking lot of the Best Western on Hancock Street in Quincy, and the answer to the last question is I'm fine." Joe looked in his rearview mirror and saw some dried blood on his neck. "But it was a little scary. He had a big knife at my throat and he asked a lot of questions. But it was obvious he didn't know who I was."

"Well, that's something."

"But there could be a problem." Declan waited. "He was watching the building when we left yesterday." Joe could hear Declan suck in his breath. "He saw Charlie and Ezra."

"Shit!"

"Yeah, I know."

"But you're okay, right?"

"Well, he threatened pretty much to cut my head off."

"You know we're working on the theory he can't kill before November 9th, so you were probably safe."

"Because it's still a theory I wasn't going to risk antagonizing him" Joe said. "He still could have messed me up pretty bad. Besides, I don't think when Joe Finn returns from the multiverse or wherever the hell he is, that he wants to wake up with one eye missing."

"Good point," Declan said. "Still, whereas he doesn't know who you really are, that means we are still holding all the cards because we know when he is going to try and kill next."

Joe thought about it for a minute. "Maybe."

"Maybe? Why maybe?"

"Think about it, Detective, if we know when a killing is going to take place, but don't know where it's going to happen or who the victim will be, are we really holding all the cards?"

Silence. "Dectective, you there?"

"Yeah. You make a good point."

More silence.

"What else is bothering you, Detective?"

"Charlie," he said. "What does he know about her?"

"I told him that she was your girlfriend."

"So he doesn't know how she's involved with the murders?"

"It didn't appear so."

"Well, that's good."

"Ummm…"

"What?"

"He knows Charlie has *somewhat* of a connection," Joe replied.

"What do you mean?" Declan asked. "Why would he think that?"

"He knows Ezra is her son."

"Ahh, damn it!"

CHAPTER SEVENTEEN

South Boston, Massachusetts
Thursday, October 21, 2021

It had been two weeks since Ian Kincaid pushed an ice-pick against her lower spine, but every day Ali Pendleton thinks she can still feel the sharp point of it pressing against her back. She knows it's a phantom pain, but that does little to alleviate the dread that courses through her body 24/7.

Ali has become a prisoner in her own mind, barely stepping outside the door more than a few times, mainly to pick up a Door Dash delivery left on her stoop. After the encounter she immediately took down the website, abruptly discontinued her podcast without explanation, refused to answer the emails overflowing in her inbox, and ignored all text messages. The only one she felt bad about was the constant stream of messages from Ezra, but she just couldn't bring herself to talk with him, less it put him in harm's way. She even phoned Detective Maroney several times but always hung up after the first ring, sure that the killer was tapping her phone. Her landlady had knocked a few times asking if she was alright. Ali merely responded that she was fine, just fighting a flu bug.

But Ali Pendleton was light years from fine. Her eating habits were terrible; sometimes days would pass where the only nourishment was a can of watery Campbell's soup. She had started to lose weight, her skin was ashen, and this morning she found more than a few strands of hair on her brush. She constantly peeked through drawn blinds, always expecting to see a car parked across the street, the engine running and the inside illuminated by nothing more than a cigarette that the killer is dragging on. And each day it becomes more and more obvious to Ali what is happening; after months of writing about countless brutal murders and insane killers stalking their victims, she is now trapped in her very own horror movie.

There appeared to be no way out of the nightmare, or was there? She looked down at her arms and wrists, the thin red lines still visible where the steak knife passed over her skin. Not deep enough to be fatal, but deep enough to give Ali an indication of what it might feel like in order to finally get some much-needed rest.

Her thoughts of eternal rest were quickly scattered by the knocking on her front door.

"Ali," cried the frantic voice of Danny Bolton on the other side of the door. "Are you in there? Open up!" She closed her eyes to try and shut out the pounding. But it was no use.

"C'mon, Ali... we need to talk. Weird things have been happening."

You don't know the half of it, she thought to herself. But she knew he wasn't going away. She went over, unlocked the door and moved back into the darkened apartment.

A moment later Danny, hearing the lock open, entered the apartment. "Jesus, Ali," he exclaimed. "What are you, a friggin' vampire?" His hand found a switch on the wall and he turned it on, shocked at what he saw. Ali sat in a chair, her knees pulled up to her chin.

"Christ, you look terrible," he said. "What the hell is going on...? Why haven't you been answering my texts?"

"I just want to be left alone."

Danny exhaled loudly. "Well that's just great. While you're doing your Howard Hughes act there's been strange goings-on down at Police HQ."

Ali lifted her head slightly. "Strange... how?"

"This big cop, Maloney...."

"Maroney."

"Whatever. He's been checking everyone's computer logs. I think he knows there's a leak."

"Is there a trail to you he can pick up?"

"I don't think so."

"Then stop worrying." She put her head back down. "There are bigger issues to worry about."

"What! Bigger than me ending up on Riker's Island as a cellmate to Big Bubba! What could be worse than that?" No response.

"Hello?"

"The guy who murdered all those girls paid me a visit," Ali said slowly. "Told me to end my podcast."

Danny went pale. "You have to be kidding? Then he thought for a moment. "Did he ask about where you got the information? Should I change my name? Should I go into witness protection? Should I ….?"

"Just shut up, will you!"

Danny stared at Ali, his face now sad. "I'm sorry, Ali... always thinking about myself." She shook her head.

"Forget it. You better leave; best not to be seen with me."

Danny looked at her for a moment, and then nodded. "Ok." He turned for the door.

"Danny?"

He turned to look at her. "Yeah?"

"Thanks for everything... Be careful."

"You, too."

Then he left Ali alone in the dark. And somehow he knew he'd never see her again.

* * * * *

While Ali Pendleton struggled to crawl out of her dark hole of despair, up in Boston Police HQ Declan Maroney was sitting in the fifth floor office of Deputy Chief Frank Roberts, who was walking back and forth behind his desk like a caged beast. Declan sat calmly on the couch, his legs crossed and arm draped over the back. He wondered to himself if the Chief's head was about to explode. And if it did; what would it look like?

"I'm telling you, Dec," he said, running his hand nervously through his hair. "Something has to break. It's been over six weeks since the first girl was found and we got squat. The Mayor, the press, Christ even my wife, is on me like ugly on a gorilla!"

"I hear you Chief, and we're going full force on this. But this guy's no crack amateur; it's not his first rodeo."

"Not making me feel any better, Dec. Try harder." Chief Roberts stopped and turned to Declan. "What about that broad with the pondcast? She seemed to have no problem coming up with theories."

"It's a podcast, Chief, and it would appear her theory on this being a copy-cat killer holds water. Can't deny the similarities. But for whatever reason, she stopped doing them."

Declan watched Chief Roberts continue to pace, muttering to himself. He knew he had to appease him somehow or somebody is going to come up with the bright idea to get the Feds involved, which was the last thing in the world he wanted to happen. But it still involved some tip-toeing.

"There is a slight possibility we may have a lead." The Chief stopped again.

"Please, God almighty, give me *something* to throw to the jackals!"

"We have someone of interest in mind, who might be worth watching closely."

"Great... who?"

"Well, I'd rather not say at this time. As you know from the podcasts, there's a leak somewhere in the department and I don't want this person spooked." Though Declan knew he already was.

"You can't tell me? I'm the goddamn Deputy Chief," he roared. Declan leaned forward on the couch, keeping his voice level.

"I know that sir, and with all due respect, it would be a nightmare for the department, and you, sir, personally, if the press knew we had a suspect but somehow the word got out due to a departmental leak and our guy beat feet to Aruba, or Gibraltar, or wherever." Chief Roberts thought about it for a minute. It kind of made sense. Sort of.

"I guess I see your point," he said slowly. Declan had him hooked; now he just had to reel him in.

"Give me two weeks and I think this will all play out in our favor."

"Two weeks?"

"Two weeks."

A slight pause and then Chief Roberts sat down heavily in his chair. "Okay, Dec... two weeks. Don't let me down."

"I won't Chief." He got up and headed for the door, thinking to himself glumly that it was really only 13 days.

CHAPTER EIGHTEEN

Boston, Massachusetts
Monday, October 25, 2021

The killer thought to himself, "You know, if Ian Kincaid weren't such a great writer he'd make an excellent spy." He laughed to himself as he traveled northbound on Route 93 heading for Boston, just passing the famed painted gas tanks.

Up ahead, maybe three car lengths ahead, Ian could still see Charlie Mitchell's blue Toyota Camry. He'd been trailing her since she left her apartment some 20 minutes ago. It was important to know what role she played in what was developing. Was it a major role, a minor role? Either way, she was definitely in play. How could she not be as the main squeeze of the cop that was trying to stop him, and the mother of electricity boy, though what his part was in this drama was still undetermined. As was that of Mr. Joe Finn. He seemed harmless enough, but Ian was still bothered by a tingle, like a small electrical charge, that he felt while he was in the backseat of his car talking with him. Might be something... might not. To be continued.

Charlie's car turned off the exit and then took a left turn towards Boston Medical Center. Ian followed close behind. As they approached the sprawling brick buildings that made up Boston Medical Center, past the cardboard houses and filthy tents of the street people who made the area their home sweet home, Ian saw Charlie's car pull into a lot marked "Employees Only."

"Hmm," he thought. "Maybe a doctor?" Looking around he quickly found a spot on the street and pulled in next to a fire hydrant. He knew he was certain to get a ticket but he didn't care. A month from now when the City of Boston sends out a bill to Mr. Ian Kincaid, let the poor guy try to figure out when he parked beside a hydrant in Roxbury.

Ian could see the lot from where he (illegally) parked, and he saw Charlie exit the car and walk towards the gate. Ian glanced in his rearview mirror and saw the blonde hair, goatee and mustache of Allan Simpson, the last man on earth Bridget Dines saw before the light in her eyes faded out. He was glad he hadn't tossed them after that fun night. Ian couldn't take the chance that she might be involved enough to know who he really was.

Ian got out of his car and followed Charlie up the steps to the front entrance of the hospital. When they both entered the lobby she greeted the security guard on duty and then headed down a flight of stairs. Ian got close enough to read the sign pointing down the stairs, which said "Morgue."

"Now that's interesting," he thought to himself. He stayed at the top of the stairs and waited a few moments until after Charlie went through the door. Then, he went down the stairs and through the door. He exited out into a long hallway lit by overhead fluorescent lights. He could hear the drip ...drip ... drip of water behind one of the doors. He walked over and smiled when he read the name Dr. C. Mitchell. While putting two and two together—Charlie Mitchell must be the Medical Examiner on the murders—the door suddenly sprung open and a fast-moving Charlie, carrying a plastic coffee mug, slammed directly into a shocked Ian Kincaid, who then tumbled back on to the floor.

"Oh, I am so sorry," Charlie blurted out. "Are you okay?" She reached down to help the man to his feet.

"No, no, entirely my fault.... I shouldn't have been standing there."

"Can I help you with something?" she asked.

"I guess I got off on the wrong floor on the elevator," the man said sheepishly. "I was looking for the lab to have some blood work done."

Charlie looked at him closely. Something felt off. But she smiled and said, "Actually, it's just off the lobby. Right through those doors at the end of the hall and up one flight. Can't miss it."

The man patted his chest appreciably and bowed his head slightly. "So many thanks." And he turned and left. Charlie watched him go through the door, remembering while she watched him exit that there was no elevator to this level.

Charlie got home about 6:00pm that evening, not really giving much thought to what happened that morning. She was exhausted and put her keys in a ceramic bowl on a table next to the front door. She kicked off her shoes and put her bag on the couch.

"Ezra, you around?"

"In the kitchen making dinner," came the reply. Charlie smiled and walked into the kitchen where she saw Ezra stirring a pot of pasta on the stove.

"Smells great… give me a much needed hug," she said, arms outstretched. He put down the spoon and walked over, embracing his mom warmly… just as a shock wave made him convulse and he staggered back, the image dancing in his head.

"Ezra! Are you okay?" she cried. "What just happened?"

Ezra shook his head slowly and looked at his frightened mom. "Who did you touch today?"

It was the same question Declan asked when Charlie got him on the phone to tell him what happened.

"C'mon Dec... you know what I do for a living," Charlie answered. "Everyone I touched today was dead."

"You're sure?"

"That they were dead?"

"No... no, that that was all you came in contact with?"

"Of course I'm...."

"What? Charlie?"

"The blonde guy," she remembered.

"What blonde guy?" Declan said.

"This morning, outside my office. I was coming out of my office and I accidentally knocked over a gentleman who was standing outside my door… said he was lost."

"What did he look like," Declan asked, his voice frantic.

"Blonde hair, goatee and mustache."

Declan thought for a moment, his breathing getting heavy. "Bridget Dines," he said.

"Who?" asked Charlie.

"The first murdered girl," he replied. "The bartender we interviewed said the guy she was with at the bar had blonde hair and a blonde goatee and mustache."

Charlie felt the blood rush from her face. "Oh my God, do you think…."

"It's the only thing that makes sense. Listen Charlie, be careful. I have to call Joe and give him an update. It's getting near the end game. Stay safe."

"You, too," Charlie responded, but Declan had already hung up.

CHAPTER NINETEEN

Bridgewater, Massachusetts
November 6, 2021

Some 30 miles south of Boston sits Bridgewater State University, a well-respected state run college that specializes in educating future teachers. Mary DiCicco, a pretty 29-year old brunette from Pittsfield, Massachusetts, was one of the students. She had always dreamed of teaching kindergarten. But that dream was snuffed out last night underneath the seats at the school's football stadium. That's where the campus police found her savaged body.

Whereas BSU is a state school, the Massachusetts State Police were called in to handle the case. Which is why Steve DiFillipo, a State Police Detective, Declan and Charlie were looking down at the body of Mary in the Medical Examiner's Office at MSP headquarters in Framingham, Massachusetts.

"We knew you were working on similar cases in the city," DiFillipo said. "So we thought you'd want to take a look."

"Appreciate that," Declan answered, still looking at the body. DiFillipo handed him a photo.

"Plus, this was written on the wall." Declan glanced at the photo, where he could see writing spray painted on a wall near the body.

Jack The Ripper LIVES!

Declan looked once again, but said nothing. The photo pretty much told him what he needed to know. But he wanted to hear it from Charlie.

"Charlie, what do you think?" She leaned in closer to examine the wounds. What she saw was that her throat had been slashed, her nose hung from her face by pieces of cartilage, her breasts were sliced, part of the skin on both legs was missing... as was her heart.

"Charlie?"

She shook her head. "It's a different killer," she answered.

"How can you be so sure?" DiFillipo asked raising his eyebrows.

"This is the work of an amateur in a great hurry," she said. "At least based on what we saw in the first four victims. You can tell by how ragged and helter-skelter the slashing is."

"What about the message; you said he always left writing behind?" DiFillipo said.

Declan shook his head. "Wrong message. Your killer somehow found out there were messages left, but we tried to keep what they were under wraps. This guy was just guessing."

"Guess this is still my case then."

"Sorry, Bro," Declan said. "Good luck."

Fortunately luck was on the side of Detective Steve DiFillipo of the Massachusetts State Police. Less than 24 hours after finding the victim an arrest was made thanks to something the killer never had to worry about in the 1800s; a fingerprint. The next day police arrested one Bruno Valente at his apartment in Whitman, Massachusetts, where they found several bloody knives, posters of Jack the Ripper on the walls… and poor Mary DiCicco's heart in a jar in the refrigerator.

CHAPTER TWENTY

Gloucester, Massachusetts
Wednesday, November 8, 2021
The night before

It was just a little before midnight, but Joe Finn wasn't tired. As he sat in his second floor cramped office over a barber shop on a pier in Gloucester, he could look out his window and see the flickering lights of dozens of buoys strewn about Gloucester Harbor. It was a cloudy, moonless night and already a stiff chilling breeze was whipping in off the water. He sat in his chair; his office illuminated only by a small desk lamp, and sipped his third Jack Daniels of the night.

Putting the glass down and savoring the burning sensation in his chest, he glanced around the office and wondered to himself just who Joe Finn was. There were a few photos on the wall. There was one with Joe surrounded by smiling youngsters in baseball uniforms. And there was another of Joe proudly holding up a baseball at Fenway Park. Joe looked at the corner of his desk and he could see the ball, now placed protectively in a plastic case, a small placard on it reading: "Home Run by Rafael Devers; June 15, 2021."

There were no family photos, no pictures of Joe with maybe his wife—if there was a wife. Oddly enough, in the past couple of months his office phone hadn't rung even once, nor did he have any visitors. It must be a lonely life. Would Joe Finn really want it back?

Joe knew in his heart how this was going to play out tomorrow; just like it played out in 1921, 1954, and 1987; with him failing miserably. It was like that movie he watched the other night with some actor named Bill Murray, about the same thing happening over and over again, and little control on how to stop it from happening. The thought depressed him and he downed what was left in his glass.

Sure, he had come close in the past. He no longer needed newspaper clippings from the BPL, as over the last week or so past lives and incarnations have slowly been coming back to him, emerging from the darkness that had been his memories, where they had previously lay dormant.

In 1921, as a prison guard in Spokane, Joe was witness to a slew of murders. He suspected the man who was involved in the executions carried out on the prison's Death Row. But he could not prove it. In 1954, Joe was a security guard at a stockyard outside Chicago, in the small town of Naperville. With a relatively small population, the town was understandably spooked by a series of vicious murders. As a security guard on the night shift, he had seen one of the workers coming and going late at night. He thought it suspicious and one night followed the guy. But when he rounded a corner he felt a knife to his throat and a warning that maybe he wanted to pursue another line of work. Frightened (and ashamed) that's just what Joe did.

And finally, in 1987, as a Detective in Pittsburgh, there were several murders revolving around the production of a low-budget slasher movie called *The Undertaker & His Pals*. It seemed that fiction and real-life were morphing together as the leading lady, script girl and one of the wardrobe gals, all inside six weeks, were found brutally murdered. Needless to say, the macabre goings-on was great PR for the film (it was the highest-grossing independent film in 1987), but Joe always suspected the director, who was a real sleaze ball. But again, there was not enough to bring him in. Joe had failed three times, four if you counted that ill-fated chase down the London alley in 1888.

Conjuring up all his past failures, and the total number of victims as a result, only depressed him more and more. But as Joe reached for the nearly-empty Jack Daniels, his phone rang. The first thought that came to mind was, "Who would be calling this late at night?" But when he saw who it was, he wasn't surprised.

"Hey, Detective. You're up late."

"I could say the same for you." Joe heard glass tinkling over the phone and wondered if Declan was pretty much doing what he was doing. Trying not to think about tomorrow. "You heard what happened at the college the other day?" Declan inquired.

"Yeah," Joe said. "Sounded terrible."

"To say the least. But not our man." The line went silent for a minute or so.

"Detective?"

"Yeah?"

"You know I've been through this before?"

"I do."

"And then you know how it always ends. Which means now I'll have the blood…"

"Stop!" Declan commanded. "Do not go there. You didn't put this shit into play."

189

"But maybe if I hadn't chased him down that alley…"

"Then he would have kept on killing in London."

"I guess. Still…."

"Joe, listen, we don't know how tomorrow is going to play out," Declan said, keeping his voice even. "We'll hope for the best and deal with the worst. All we can do."

"I know," Joe responded, although not too convincingly. "I'll see you tomorrow."

"Until tomorrow," Dec replied and hung up.

Joe Finn held the dead phone in his hand and all he could think to say was, "Happy Groundhog Day."

CHAPTER TWENTY-ONE

Boston, Massachusetts
Tuesday, November 9, 2021
The Day Of

"You hear him howling around your kitchen door
You better not let him in
Little old lady got mutilated late last night
Werewolves of London again."

--Warren Zevon

Predictable was the only word Ian could think of as he peered through his window blinds only to see the Boston Police cruiser sitting opposite his apartment building. And he didn't need to look to figure out there was also likely one watching the back door of the apartment building. This is precisely why he made sure earlier that the door to his building's roof was unlocked. He had to laugh as he asked himself; "Do these fools think they can stop fate?"

Pulling on his leather jacket and donning a Red Sox cap, he checked his pocket to make sure he had what he needed and then took the two flights of stairs up to the roof. Opening the door a cold blast of air hit him, but he ignored it and crossed over to the adjacent building where he knew, for whatever reason, the roof door was never locked. Once inside he took the stairs down to the front door, pulled the cap down tighter on his forehead and ventured casually out onto Commonwealth Avenue and headed for Charlesgate East, where an Uber—most deserving of a five star rating—would deliver him to his final destination.

* * * * *

While Ian Kincaid was on his way across town chatting with an Uber driver named Morris about the New England Patriots' season, Detective Declan Maroney sat at his desk at Police Headquarters, totally demoralized. Across from him, Joe Finn, also seated, was equally depressed.

"You know," Declan said, squeezing the life out of a stress ball with his right hand, "For the past I don't know how many years as a homicide detective, I never knew when the next murder was going to happen." He moved the ball to his left hand. "But now I know *when* and likely by *who*, and I'm still totally frustrated."

"I know the feeling," Joe Finn said. "Helpless." Then after giving it some thought, he asked, "You have cars watching Kincaid's apartment, right?"

"Yeah, front and back," Declan replied. "They just checked in and said he entered his apartment about two hours ago and hasn't left since." He shook his head. "That makes no sense. We have the date correct, don't we. November 9th?"

Joe nodded. "There's no question about that." Declan squeezed the ball harder, just as the front desk Sergeant came over and dropped an envelope in front of him. "Hey, Dec, meant to give this to you," the Sergeant said. "It was dropped off at the front desk earlier today."

Declan looked at the plain white envelope with his name elegantly written on the front. He opened it, took out the paper, unfolded it and read what was written. Disgusted he threw it down on the desk. "Friggin' A!" he exclaimed. "The balls on this guy! He's not even waiting until he commits the crime to leave us letters. Son of a bitch!"

Joe turned the letter around and read the initials. Something wasn't right. Declan could see the strange look on Joe's face. "What?" Joe looked up at him.

"The last original victim was Mary Kelly ... MK."

"And..." said Declan. "What of it?"

Joe turned the paper back towards Declan. "Look at these initials." Declan did as he was asked, but within moments his face turned crimson. "*Motherfu....!*" Declan pulled out his phone and frantically started calling. It went right to voicemail. "Shit!"

"Do you know where she is?" Joe asked. Declan had to think for a moment.

"She said she was working late tonight." He leaped out of his chair and grabbed his coat. "Come on, hurry!" Declan moved so fast that the breeze blew the paper off his desk and on to the floor where it landed face up with the letters:

CM

It was just a little after 8:00pm and Dr. Charlie Mitchell was the only one still at work at the City Morgue. Cursing herself for forgetting her phone charger, her now dead phone sat useless on her desk. A few more reports to finish, pick up some late dinner for her and Ezra, and then to bed. She had arrived at her office early, a little before 7:00AM, and fatigue was winning out. She pushed back from her desk and stretched her arms out, hearing the popping in her neck muscles. But she also heard something that was definitely not joints creaking.

The sound had come from the morgue. Which she thought strange as she was told she was the last person and to lock up when she was finished. She heard the sound again. More curious than frightened, she walked out of her office and went down the hall. She noticed right away that the door to the morgue was open, which she found equally strange because she was sure she had closed it. The room was dark as she peered in, and this time the only sound being a steady drip of a faucet in one of the sinks. The glow of the red emergency exit light shone eerily on the row of stainless steel tables. Making her way carefully over to the sink to shut off the faucet, she was startled by the overhead fluorescent lights suddenly bursting to life. She gasped and used a table to steady herself. And then she heard the voice from behind her.

"Hello, Charlie."

* * * * *

Since the City Morgue was only several blocks from Police Headquarters, Declan and Joe made it in nothing flat. They tried the front door and found it locked. "Damn!" Declan yelled. "You stay here, I'll try around the back!" he told Joe, taking off as fast as he could. When he got to the back of the building, he could see the glass door in the back alley was also locked. But that wasn't going to stop him. Looking around he found a brick and with one mighty slam, fueled by an adrenaline rush, the glass shattered, allowing Declan to reach in and unlock the door.

* * * * *

Charlie backed up slowly as Ian Kincaid, a long ugly-looking knife held at his side, moved slowly towards her.

"You know, Charlie," he said casually. "I have always been fascinated by your job, and perhaps I dare say; even envious. To be able to actually have free reign to cut and dissect the human form, it must be a real rush. Is it?"

Charlie kept backing up but was running out of room. "I'll scream," she warned. Ian seemed unfazed.

"Yes, you could," he said matter-of-factly, "But I am not sure anyone would hear you." He pointed at the drawers. "Certainly not these poor souls." Ian advanced closer. "Did you ever think to yourself what it would be like to be lying on one of these tables?" he asked, tapping the knife on the steel. "To look up at the person who is about to delve into your insides? Talk about the ultimate violation."

"You're crazy."

Ian shrugged, "History would seem to have made that determination. Did you happen to read about what I did to my fifth victim, poor Mary Jeannette Kelly?" When Charlie didn't answer he continued. "I slashed her throat, cut off her nose and breasts, pulled out her entrails, cut out her heart, and then, just for fun, skinned her body."

Charlie could feel the bile rising in her throat. Making a last ditch effort she attempted to make a run for the inner office, but Ian was on her like a cat, his powerful arms around her shoulders and holding the sharp knife to her throat. His hot breath whispered in her ear. "Shall we begin?"

"Drop the knife, Kincaid. It's over."

Ian turned around, still holding Charlie in front of him as they now faced Declan, his gun held out straight. Ian seemed unfazed by the turn of events.

"Detective Maroney, how nice to see you again." He tightened his grip on Charlie. "But you know how this ends, how it always ends."

"It ends with either you in prison for life or a bullet in your head."

"If you don't mind, I think I'll take door number three," he said with a small laugh. "The one that has you dropping your gun before I put just a little... more... pressure on this knife." And he proceeded to do so, but only just enough to have a thin stream of blood drip down Charlie's neck. She winced at the pain.

"Stop!" Declan shouted, knowing he didn't have a clear shot without possibly hitting Charlie. "I'm putting it down," he said, laying the gun on the table.

"Stop?" Ian repeated. "Stop? Can a fish stop swimming? Can a bird stop flying? Can you stop fate?" And with that he drew the blade across Charlie's throat.

"No!" Declan screamed racing forward. But before he could take two steps he heard a roar and Ian Kincaid's forehead disappeared in a gory spray of blood, bone and gray matter. The knife dropped to the floor, as did Ian and Charlie, only to reveal Joe Finn standing in the door of the inner office, the gun still smoking in his shaking hands.

They both raced to over to Charlie who was bleeding heavily and gasping for breath, Joe grabbed a towel and applied pressure to the wound. He looked up at Joe. "How did you get in?"

"Well," he replied. "It appears that one of Joe Finn's unique skills, which I was unaware of, is the ability to pick locks."

"Thank God!" Declan said, looking down at Charlie. Joe took out his phone to call 911.

"Detective, you know it's important that we not let her be the fifth victim, don't you?" Declan nodded.

"We're not going to let that happen," he said.

* * * * *

Less than three hours later Declan and Joe Finn stood at Charlie's bedside at Boston Medical Center. As luck would have it, there was an ambulance parked outside the building, on a break, when the call came through. They had Charlie to the hospital in no time, thankfully.

Declan stood at the side of the bed and looked down at her, still unconscious, her neck wrapped up to hide the dozens of stitches needed to close the gaping wound. She had lost a great amount of blood, but the doctors said she was going to make it. The loop was now severed.

"We saved her, Joe," Declan said. "Or should I now call you Frederick Abberline?"

"What?"

"I said, should I now call you Frederick..." but he stopped when he turned and saw a look of confusion on Joe Finn's face.

"Who's Frederick Abberline?" he asked. "My name is Finn; Joe Finn." Now he looked more scared than confused, and Declan felt his heart skip when he noticed Joe no longer sported a scar over his eyebrow. Joe's eyes darted around the room.

"Is this a hospital?" his voice now panicked. "Where am I? Who are you? Why am I here?"

All Declan Maroney could do was stare at the frightened man. "Oh no," were the only words that passed his lips.

EPILOGUE

Quincy, Massachusetts
Monday, August 28, 2054

At 73-years of age, Declan Maroney stood on the eighth floor balcony of his apartment in a senior housing complex in Quincy, drinking a cup of coffee and admiring the sun setting over the Boston skyline off in the distance. It had been a hot August day but this high up there was always a breeze. Declan didn't mind living by himself; kind of liked the solitude. He retired from the BPD 10 years ago and he was enjoying life.

But even more than 30 years later, it was hard not to think of all the people that affected his life for almost three months back in the day. His old partner, Billy "Bear" Montour, left the Boston Police and moved up to the reservation outside Montreal a year after the killings. Last Declan heard he even became their Chief of Police. After the terrifying run-in with Ian Kincaid, Ali Pendleton did as she was told and signed off on her last podcast. Two months later she hooked up with the guitarist in a punk-rock band playing the Hard Rock outside Fenway Park and hit the road with him, never to be seen again. He guessed writing about killers, and then almost becoming a victim of one, was too much for her. Declan couldn't blame her.

Needless to say, the press had a field day trying to figure out why a respected best-selling writer had suddenly turned serial killer. A few years later NETFLIX made a movie based on the murder case, with Colin Farrell playing the killer. The production company paid Declan a hefty sum to serve as a "consultant."

As for Joe Finn, Declan had been tempted to reach out to him since the day he left Charlie's hospital room, totally confused. But he chose not to, unable to figure out how to explain to the poor guy how his life had been hijacked. Better to let sleeping dogs lie.

Declan walked over to his CD player and hit "play." Soon the melodic sounds of Paul Simon & Art Garfunkel filled the room.

He walked back into his apartment and thought of Charlie Mitchell, closing the balcony door behind him. Charlie had moved to Tampa 20 years ago, wanting to be closer to her son. Ezra turned out to be a pretty good writer, and by the time he was 30 published his first book; a best-seller. The subject: of course, serial killers. Simon & Art Garfunkel filled the room.

"Hello darkness, my old friend..."

Declan loved this CD, all their hits, and it seemed like he played it almost every day. Just couldn't get enough of it. But this was his favorite song.

"I've come to talk with you again..."

Thinking of Charlie, Declan remembered it had been awhile since he had dropped her an email to see how things were going in Florida. He sat down at his computer, and as he started to reach for the mouse to turn on the screen, he pulled back his hand as a piercing pain erupted in his head.

"Aarrghh!!", he cried out in agony, holding his head. But as quickly as the pain came it subsided. Declan took a deep breath as he tried to collect his thoughts. He reached out again for the mouse but stopped suddenly. He wasn't sure what to do next, or even how to turn on the..... *the what?* He stared at the machine in front of him, trying hard to remember what it was, or why it was in his apartment. Another bolt of pain erupted, but again quickly subsiding. Now Declan was breathing heavy. He could hear music. Somebody singing... no, two people singing. But he didn't recognize the song.

He reached into his back pocket where he felt a wallet. Quickly pulling it from his pocket he pulled out a plastic card that said VISA and read the name. Suddenly, Declan's face no longer showed confusion, and as a matter of fact a small smile started to appear. He got up from his chair and went into the bathroom. Gazing into the mirror on the medicine cabinet, he smiled at the image staring back at him.

"Hello, old friend," he said. "A little more gray perhaps, but to be expected. Still, looking in pretty good shape." He listened for a moment to the music drifting in from the other room. "Ah, Simon & Garfunkel... our favorite."

Using his breath, he fogged up the mirror and with his index finger traced out three letters. Then he stood back and smiled while admiring his penmanship.

MAN

April 1, 2021 – January 23, 2022

Also by Stephen A. White

Available on Amazon

Time Passages
American Pop
The Voice of Rage & Ruin
Murder at 33 RPM: A Rock 'n Roll Horror Story
Ersillia: Love & Loss (with Kathleen Anderson)
On Air: My 50-Year Love Affair with Radio (with Jordan Rich)
Love Between the Pages (with Connie Thamert)
Front Row Center: How I Met Everyone (with Allan Dines)

From Steve White Publishing
Available on Amazon

Novels and Autobiographies

There and Back Again (Dorothy Roberts)
Flanagan's Fall (Karen Maguire)
Portals (PJ Yovino)
St. Augustine's Finger (Frank X. Roberts)
Books/Bookmarks Through the Ages (Frank X. Roberts)
The Eye's Plain Version (Frank X. Roberts)
The Twin Towers: A Poem for Children (Cam Giangrande)
Young at Heart (Steve Yanofsky)
Flight of Four (Robert Sprenger)
Michael Kirst Biography (Richard Jung)
50 Years of Celebrity Chatter (Bill Diehl)
The Dorothy Sonnets (Frank X. Roberts)

Business and Self-Help

Investing...Without the Bull (Robert Stabile)
How to Avoid the Four-Headed Monster (Patrick J. Kelleher)
A Guide to Excellent (and Successful) Aging (Mark H. Friedman)
Inner Moron Demons (Larry J. Feldman)
Freedom Thru Fitness (Matthew Sinosky)
Frustrated & Overcharged (David R. Leng)
The 10 Laws of Insurance Attraction (David R. Leng)

Turning Premiums into Profits (David R. Leng)
Insured to Fail (David R. Leng)
The Private Club General Managers Big Game Playbook
(Toni Shibayama*)*
The Big Game Playbook: Don't Let The Rising Cost of Workers' Comp
Crush Your Business
(Toni Sibayama)

www.SteveWhitePublishing.com

Made in the USA
Middletown, DE
18 September 2022